BEACH MY LIFE

Book 3 Hawaii Heat

By

Jamie K. Schmidt

To my MTBs who when I told them that 2018 was going to be the year of self-publishing dangerously (YOSPD), didn't have me committed. Thank you, Denise, Gail, Heidi, Jane, Jamie B, Jamie P., Jennifer, Katy, Stephanie, and Tracy, for always having my back and being my most trusted bitches.

Table of Contents

Chapter One

Joely Anderson walked out on the lanai to take a deep breath before she puked.

People were pigs.

As the head maid in the newly renovated and very popular Palekaiko Beach Resort, she thought she had seen it all. A mountain of sand in the shower? No problem. Leftover food rotting in eighty-degree temperature? Been there, done that. She'd even came across a dead body once. That nice gentleman, Mr. Frank, in room 301 had died peacefully in his sleep at the ripe old age of ninety.

Drunks were the worse, though. Drunks who didn't care how bad they left their bathrooms should have a special place in hell. Her walkie beeped, and she toggled on the button on her headset as she gulped in the fresh ocean air.

"Yeah?"

"Is everything all right?"

Joely straightened up, and self-consciously tugged down her uniform.

"Why?" She was on the fourth floor. Peering around the grounds, she didn't see the head of security, Holt Kawena, but she wasn't surprised he had eyes on her. He had eyes everywhere.

"I was wondering if we had a code one-hundred on our hands."

That was a polite way of saying he hoped there wasn't another dead body in the room.

"Nope, just smells like it." She grimaced. "Where are you, anyway?" Looking all over the property, she ignored the beautiful

5

blue ocean, the white sand beach and the palm trees that swayed in the brisk Maui breeze. She could see guests heading to and from the restaurant. Some had already situated themselves by the pool, even though the action over there didn't really get good until after lunch. But she didn't see Holt, who was probably wearing his signature khakis and a mild patterned Hawaiian shirt.

She would have recognized his muscular build anywhere. He was the kind of guy that the postcard photographers would take a picture of when he was out on his surfboard. Joely missed a lot of waves watching him. Holt had muscles that looked like he spent his time bench pressing smart cars.

When she first got hired, Kai and Hani, two of the bell staff, told her he was ex-special forces, and she made an ass out of herself thanking Holt for his service. Holt just looked like a member of Seal Team Six. He wasn't ever in the armed forces.

Joely had a history of making an ass out of herself with him, so she just stopped trying to catch his eye. Then, there was the prostitution scandal—that she had been totally innocent of—and ever since then Holt watched her like a hawk. It was like he thought just because he didn't catch her this time, didn't mean she wasn't up to something.

Her life wasn't that interesting now, and that was just the way she liked it. Still, sometimes she wished she had a little more fun in her life. Her friends Amelia and Michaela were always trying to get her to go to Paint Night or Plant Night or Drink Night with them.

And while that was good, inevitably the night would end and so would Joely's reprieve. Amelia would go back home to Dude—her husband, without a care in the world. The next morning Michaela would wake up next to her husband, Marcus, and they would plot their next business venture. On the other hand, Joely would get out

6

of bed and go scrub toilets for most of the day, when she wasn't working on staffing issues.

"I was just passing by," Holt said, jarring her out of her thoughts. "when I saw you bolt out onto the lanai."

"I'm thinking about jumping," she muttered, eyeing the ground below her. Nothing but plumeria bushes and pavement.

"Don't. We can't afford the extra staff to clean up the mess."

Joely snorted. The hotel was doing well. They probably could afford it. The renovations were almost done, and Holt's uncle, Tetsuo, had found another property to harass.

"Speaking of messes, I guess it's time to do the nasty." She sighed. Then winced when he gave a small cough that could have been laughter. Not how she meant it. Not that Holt ever even thought of her like that anyway. Holding her breath, she went back inside. There was a lot of bleach in her future. As she scooped up the bedsheets off the bed, a man's wallet dropped out. Figures.

She stuffed the sheets into her bin that she left in the hallway, and then went back in to pick the wallet up off the floor.

"Hey, Holt," she said, toggling the microphone back on. "I just want to log that I picked up room 418's wallet. It fell out of the bed."

"Give me a money count just in case there is a problem."

Making a face, she opened the wallet. She hated doing that, but she hated having to defend herself against a complaint that she took money even more. When she glanced down and saw the license photo, the wallet fell out of her nerveless fingers. She must have made a noise because Holt sounded alarmed.

"What is it?"

"I have to leave," she whispered, and ran out of the room.

"Talk to me," he barked.

Whipping the headset off, she tossed the communication unit in her cart. Locking the door with shaking fingers, Joely pushed the cart to the elevator. But seeing the car was already on its way up, she panicked and bolted for the back stairs.

He found her. She wasn't sure how he did. But five years later, after reconstructive surgery and a name change, it could not be coincidence that her ex-husband was staying at the same resort she was hiding out in.

Chapter Two

Holt Kawena almost plowed into the maid's cart when he rushed out of the elevator.

"Joely?" he called, but there wasn't any answer. He resisted kicking the door to 418 down, and used his master key instead. The stench punched him in the face and he couldn't blame Joely for making a run for it.

His eyes narrowed on the wallet on the floor. He strode over to it, and picked it up.

Timothy Andrews. Blond hair. Blue eyes. Age forty-five. From Minnesota. Two hundred bucks in the wallet. Three credit cards. One identification card from the Minnesota state Senate.

What was it about Mr. Andrews that made Joely cry out like a frightened kitten? Tossing the wallet on the bureau by the TV, Holt left the room, locking it behind him. If Joely wasn't here, she must have taken the stairs.

"Cami, I need you to clean the fourth floor today," he said, toggling on his microphone.

"Why not Joely?" Cami whined. "That's her floor today."

"She got sick. Room 418 needs a bio hazard suit to clean it, though."

"Ugh great."

"Sorry. Some days you're the windshield…"

"And some days, you're the bug," Cami finished with a sigh. "She better not be at the fucking beach."

Holt didn't answer, but he didn't think she was. He didn't feel badly about giving Cami the extra work. Technically, it should have come from Amelia, but Holt was worried that Amelia would come and clean the rooms instead.

Cami was a slacker, who took advantage of Joely's sweet nature. If she was one of his employees, he'd have had Cami whipped into shape or sent her packing long before now. Let her do some dirty work for a change.

Making his way to the front desk, he saw Makoa manning the desk and Kai booking excursions. "Have you seen Joely?" he asked Makoa.

"Nah, but we were going to go for a bike ride later."

Holt frowned. He didn't think there was anything between Joely and Makoa, but the idea of her wrapping her arms around him while they zoomed down the street didn't sit well with him.

"Do you have a helmet for her?"

"Nah, we're not going *motobaik*. We're going *wilwil*." Makoa made pedaling motions with his hand.

"Do you have a helmet for her?" Holt repeated.

"She got a hard head, just like me." Makoa knocked on his skull for emphasis.

Willing himself not to roll his eyes, Holt asked, "When were you going?"

"After lunch."

It wasn't even after ten yet.

"When you see her, I need to speak to her right away."

"Right away, boss." Makoa saluted him.

Holt had his doubts that Makoa would even remember this conversation, but hopefully Holt would find Joely before lunch. His next stop was her room, but he didn't expect her to answer his knock. He was tempted to use his master key there as well, but in the end just peeked in her lanai door. The blinds were closed, so that was a dead end.

Taking a walk down the path that lead to the beach, he constantly scanned both sides of the walkway, looking for a flash of her blue uniform or her strawberry blond hair.

Even if it weren't for her glorious hair, Joely would stand out in a crowd. She had long legs and a sassy smirk. He liked that she wasn't intimidated by his size and told him off when she thought he was being overbearing. He'd wanted to get to know her better, but there was something about her that set him on edge.

She was hiding something, lying to all of them. At first, he thought she was turning tricks for the tourists. Then when he caught the real prostitutes, he thought Joely might be a thief, but she didn't take any of the bait he tried to trap the maids with. Two of them failed the test and pocketed a lone diamond earring. The rest of the staff—Joely included—reported just finding one and put it in a cup in the bathroom per their rules and regulations.

Then last year, she really had been hiding something from him. Michaela had been squatting illegally in their unfinished rooms, but since Michaela went on to marry one of the owners, Holt didn't hold that against Joely.

Fishing out his sunglasses, Holt slid them over his eyes as he walked onto the Kaanapali beach. He knew this resort and the beach like the back of his hand, having grown up here when his uncle tried to get his father to give up the *paniolo* life. But while you probably could take the cowboy out of the alcoholic, you couldn't take the bottle away from him.

Striding over to where Samuel Kincaide, aka Dude, hung in his hammock, Holt had no compunctions about standing over him, even if he was the co-owner of the resort with his brother Marcus.

"You're blocking the sun, brah," Dude croaked out.

"Have you seen Joely?"

"Not my turn to watch her."

"Where's Amelia?"

"She was heading for the front desk an hour ago."

"She's not there now," Holt said, trying to maintain his patience.

When his father sold the resort to the Kincaide brothers, it was in dire need of a bulldozer. Years of neglect because Mel Kawena was a weak drunk who wouldn't stand up to his wife's brother, caused the resort to be on the edge of bankruptcy. Holt had desperately wanted to keep the resort in the family.

But his father had other ideas. Mel had taken the Kincaides' money and literally ran. Holt hadn't seen his father in over three years.

He could have blamed the millionaire *haoles*, but that would make him too much like his uncle, Tetsuo Hojo. So, he befriended them instead.

"It's not my turn to watch Amelia either," Dude said, stifling a yawn. And Amelia was his wife.

Marcus was the easier brother to deal with, but he was in California this week helping his wife with a case. They were both attorneys and practiced on the mainland as well as on the islands.

"I think we might have a problem with one of our guests. If you see either of them, tell them to call me."

"Roger dat." Dude gave him the shaka.

Walking away, Holt called Joely's cell phone again. This time, surprisingly, she answered it. "Look, it's not a good time."

"Where are you?"

Her voice was shaky and wild, and he was worried.

"I'm at Whaler's Village. I didn't want to do anything touristy, but I was afraid to stay on the resort and I was afraid to walk on the road."

He bristled at the fear he heard from her and increased his pace. It was a five-minute walk to Whaler's Village. "Where are you?" he repeated.

For a moment, he didn't think she was going to answer him, but then she spoke and he had to strain to hear her. "I'm in Trendy Topics."

Holt made a face. "Why?"

"Because the last place he'll be is in a tween pop shop."

"Senator Andrews?"

"Did you talk to him?" Her voice rose alarmingly.

"No, I saw the wallet. Calm down. I'll be right there."

"Make sure you're not followed." She hung up.

Casually looking behind him, Holt leaned up against a wooden brochure stand. He waved off the time share *wahine* and waited a few minutes. Tourists bustled by him. A few waiters darted in and out hurrying from the restaurant bars to the beach. No one was paying him any attention or tailing him, certainly no one who looked like Senator Andrews.

As Holt made his way through the beachfront and into the back of the Whaler's Village shopping mall, he continued scanning. He still didn't see anyone out of the ordinary. Bracing himself, he walked into Trendy Topics. All at once, his senses shut down in self-defense. His ears were assaulted by a loud noise that had a deep bass. Some of the kids danced to it. Taking off his sunglasses, he squinted into the darkness only to be blinded by the strobe light. The overwhelming smell of patchouli wafted into his nostrils. A hand touched his arm and he turned.

"Were you followed?" Joely asked.

Her face was so white that her freckles stood out in sharp contrast, and her green eyes were misted with tears. Holt wanted to bundle her up into his arms until color came back to her face.

"Let's get out of here." He took her by the upper arm, but was surprised when she dug her heels in.

"Are you working for him?"

"Don't be ridiculous." Holt pulled her towards the front of the store, so desperate to get out of this nightmare place that he almost ran into a bikini display.

"Where are you taking me?" she said, twisting in his grip.

He let her go and she stumbled back. "Joely." He held out his hand to her. "I can't think in this place. Let's go to the beach."

She shook her head. "I can't. He might see me."

"I'll be with you."

"I won't always be with you."

Holt sighed. "I get that you're scared. Tell me why."

Hugging herself, Joely looked around. "You won't believe me. You never believe me. Look, tell everyone I quit. If he asks for me, please just do me a favor and tell him you never saw me, that I was never here."

"Are you in trouble with the law?"

She gave a half laugh and shook her head. "See, you always think the worst."

14

"Just tell me what is going on. I'll go back and get my car. I'll meet you by the parking lot. We'll go up to D.T. Fleming and paddle out. No one will bother us."

Biting her lip, she looked around the store. "All right."

"Fifteen minutes." He tapped his watch. "Meet me in the parking lot."

She nodded.

Holt sprinted back to the Palekaiko resort. His phone rang just as he was rounding the corner into the lobby.

"Oh," Amelia said, hanging up the phone. "I was just calling you."

Amelia was a pretty blond with enough energy to fuel a dozen cars. She was their concierge and did her job well. Why she married a slacker like Dude was beyond Holt's imagination.

"Has anyone been looking for Joely?" Holt said.

"Just you." Amelia narrowed her eyes at him. "Why? What's going on?"

"I don't know yet, but she's afraid of the guy in 418. He's a Minnesota senator named Timothy Andrews. Can you reiterate with the staff that it's against company policy to give out any personal information about a staff member to a guest?"

"Sure. Is everything all right?"

Holt nodded. "It will be. But for right now, Joely and I are taking the day off."

"You are?" Amelia looked shocked.

Holt knew he didn't take time for himself ever and certainly not with Joely, but she didn't have to look so surprised. "Just keep it on the down low. I'll have my cell phone on me for emergencies, though. I'll fill Dude in on everything later."

15

"I want to be there when you do. Be careful."

He nodded, and took his keys off the peg from behind the concierge desk.

"Hey, Holt," Hani, the bell captain, said.

Looking up, Holt saw that Hani was leading a guest towards him. He wasn't surprised to recognize Senator Andrews from his driver's license photo. Assessing the man, Holt wasn't impressed. Andrews was tall, but flabby, and he had a mean look about him.

A bully.

Rising up to his full height, Holt let them come to him. "Yes?" he said, politely. Maybe he'd be able to find out why Joely was so afraid of this asshole.

"This is Senator Andrews. He's looking for someone. I didn't recognize her, but I figured you might." Hani turned to the senator. "Holt is the director of security. He knows everyone."

"Thank you," Andrews rapped out curtly. "You may go."

Hani's face was schooled in polite disinterest as he walked away, but he shot an unreadable look over his shoulder at Holt and shook his head "no" at him.

Interesting.

"What can I help you with?"

"Have you seen this woman?" Andrews shoved a picture in his face.

Plucking the picture out of the man's hand, he studied it. It was definitely Joely. He could tell that by the eyes and the freckles. But her face was fuller and her hair was brown, cut short in a severe pixie cut. It showed off her cheekbones. Her nose was different too. And in this picture, she wasn't smiling. This was not the woman who haunted his thoughts and laughed with her friends while surfing.

"No, can't say that I have. Who is she?" Holt handed the picture back to Andrews.

Andrews frowned and glared at it. "She's my wife."

Holt forced himself not to react as his stomach dropped to his shoes. "What makes you think she's here?" Out of the corner of his eye, he saw Amelia practically standing on her tip toes to get a look at the picture.

"I saw a picture on the internet of her. She was wearing a maid's uniform from this resort."

Holt nodded. "Well, I can look in our system to see if she's ever worked here."

"I would appreciate that, son."

Baring his teeth in what he hoped was a smile, Holt went around the desk where Amelia was and opened up a browser window.

"May I see?" Amelia said.

When the senator handed her the picture, Holt gave her a warning look.

"What's your wife's name, sir?" he said, watching Amelia stiffen in recognition. But she didn't say anything.

"Annie Andrews. But she might be using her maiden name Post."

Amelia watched over his shoulder as he googled Annie Post Andrews Minnesota. "I don't see anything in our system for an employee by that name."

"I'm sorry," Amelia broke in. "I didn't catch your name, sir."

"Amelia is one of the owners of the resort, and our concierge," Holt said.

"I'm Senator Timothy Andrews from Minnesota."

"I see here," Amelia said, typing information in their reservation computer, "that you checked in alone yesterday. Were you expecting your wife to come in today?"

"No," he said, brushing his hand in the air. "I haven't seen her in almost five years. We're estranged."

Amelia's lips tightened and she handed him back the photo.

Holt could confirm that there was a woman named Annie Post who married Timothy Andrews. He saw the marriage announcement. He could see if there was a divorce filed, but he'd have to put a credit card in and he didn't want to do that with the senator watching.

"Perhaps, then, she doesn't want to see you," Amelia said swiftly.

"We have unfinished business between us. I will find her." Timothy slammed his fist on the counter.

"Easy," Holt growled out. He couldn't find any police or court reports from Minnesota.

"I'm sorry. I'm just very concerned about her. She has ... mental issues. She's sick."

Holt almost went over the desk. The urge to pummel this guy senseless was strong, but he refrained himself.

"I can ask around to the other resorts," Amelia cut in. "All of our uniforms are similar."

"They are?" Timothy said, frowning.

No, they weren't, but it was possible that someone like Timothy wouldn't notice that.

18

"Let me put a note in your file that if she turns up to contact you immediately. May I see your driver's license?"

Bless her. Holt watched as Amelia typed in his driver's license number, home address.

"Phone number, please?"

She was good. That would be more than enough to search for more details.

"Thank you," she said, handing his license back to him. "Please enjoy your stay. May I recommend a tour to Molokini for some snorkeling?"

Timothy considered it, but then shook his head. "I'd like to speak to your service staff."

"It's 50% off today only," Amelia said, as if she hadn't heard him. "But the bus leaves in twenty minutes."

"Really?" He pocketed his wallet. "Does that include lunch?"

"It does."

Holt smirked in amusement as she then proceeded to charge him full price and print him out a voucher. "You can pick up the shuttle bus to Ma'alaea Harbor out front." Amelia pointed to the entrance.

"I need to go back to my room and change, but I would still like to speak with the staff when I get back."

"I'll make the arrangements," she said.

When the senator left, Amelia turned to Holt. "What the fuck is going on?"

"I'm not sure, but Joely's hiding out at Whaler's Inn, terrified of that asshole. I'm going to take her out to D.T. Fleming and see if I can get to the bottom of this. When you talk to the staff, be firm. No one tells him anything, or they answer to me."

Chapter Three

Every instinct in Joely's body was telling her to run, but she didn't know where. She couldn't risk going back to her job and her friends. If Timothy found her, he could easily overpower her and she'd be on a plane back to Minnesota before she came to.

How did he find her? She was always so careful to be in the background at the hotel events where she might be caught on camera. She never was on social media. It was too coincidental to be just a chance meeting.

"Are you going to buy something?" the sales girl asked, while chewing her gum.

"Yeah." Joely grabbed a bikini, a tote bag, and a towel. "I'll take these please."

After the sales girl rang her up, she darted into their bathroom to change. Stuffing her maid's uniform into the tote bag, she tugged on the suit. It was far too young for her, way too little, and an annoying shade of purple. It was nothing like Annie Andrews would wear. And that was the point.

Maybe she could get Holt to pack her things for her while she waited in the car. If she could get him to take her to the bank too, that would make things easier.

If she could trust him.

If he believed her.

If he ever showed up.

Glancing out the door of the shop, she still didn't see him or his car. He was late. Holt was never late.

"These too." Joely added a pair of flip flops. She wouldn't be able to run fast in them, but they stood out less than her comfortable sneakers. "And these." She plopped down a large pair of sunglasses and a wide brimmed hat.

The girl sighed as if this was all too much for her. Joely paid with her credit card, wondering if she should drain her bank account and stick with using cash. She was taking a risk that Timothy hadn't cracked her identity, but it was nearly impossible to connect Annie Post Andrews to Joely Anderson. Her identification and social security number were the best that money could buy. Her sister had seen to that.

Putting on the hat and sunglasses, Joely wrapped the towel around her waist and bustled out with some tourists. Heading towards the parking lot, she darted glances all around her. Timothy could be anywhere.

Luckily, Holt had decided to show up after all. He parked by the curb, and she eased into the passenger side of his Honda Accord. Noting the surfboards on top, a little tension eased out of her back. It would be nice to surf one last time.

"What the hell are you wearing?" Holt barked at her, as she pulled the seatbelt around her and clicked it in place.

Normally, she would have blushed and stammered being in such close proximately to him. But suddenly, she was so very tired, she just didn't give a fuck anymore. She wouldn't be seeing him again anyway, which was too damned bad.

"I couldn't wear my uniform."

"Did you put sunscreen on?" he continued.

"What? No. It wasn't on my list of things to do."

"Glove compartment. You're going to get burned to a crisp."

"We're not going to be out there that long," Joely said regretfully.

"With your skin, we don't need to."

He had a point. She pulled the sun block out and slathered it all over, trying not to get any on his leather seats.

"Did you give Amelia my notice?" Joely asked. She'd figure out how to do her back once they were on the beach. The thought of his big hands smoothing over her body made her shiver. She had a crush on him from the moment she laid eyes on him five years ago. Then he had to ruin it by accusing her of being a hooker.

"I said we were taking the day off."

"I need to leave the island. I was wondering if you could pack up my things for me and drive me to the bank so I can drain my account?"

"Why don't you tell me what's going on? I talked to Senator Andrews."

"What?" Panic coursed through her. "You what?" She looked in the backseat, suddenly positive Timothy was hiding back there waiting to jump out at her. When he wasn't there, she gripped the door handle. Holt locked the doors. With a jolt, she realized she was trapped. But a quick look out the window confirmed that they were on the way to the beach instead of going back to the resort. Forcing her hands to stay still, she clasped them in front of her. "What did you tell him?"

"He showed me an old picture of you. I told him I hadn't seen you."

Joely deflated like a balloon against the soft leather seats. "Thank you," she said weakly.

"Your husband seems eager to find you."

She bristled. "Ex-husband."

Holt nodded. "Good."

"You're damn right it's good. Of course, that little piece of paper ending our marriage didn't mean anything." She risked a glance at him under her lashes. "Or the restraining order I filed against him."

Joely knew Holt got what she was trying to say by the way his jaw clenched.

"What's he doing here looking for you now?"

Blowing out a sigh, she rested her forehead against the window. "I wish I knew." Straightening, she played with the threads in her towel. It was so cheaply made, it was already fraying. "But I can't let him find me."

"Why?" Holt said.

"He'll kill me." Joely shrugged.

Holt went white knuckled on the steering wheel. "What do you mean?"

"I mean the last time, he shattered my jaw, broke my cheekbone and smashed my nose." Joely was surprised that her voice was so calm. She felt like she was floating above the car looking down. "I married him just after high school. He was controlling, and at first I didn't know any better because he treated me like my father treated my mother. But then he wanted to run for the Senate, and he needed for me to have a college degree."

Her mind wandered to those first gloriously frightening days of attending classes on the huge state campus. She was so excited to take all the computer classes she could. She had even conned Timothy into buying her an expensive gaming rig.

"I learned a lot of things he hadn't expected me to. Freshman psych was an eye opener. I filed for divorce sophomore year and moved to on-campus housing. I got a restraining order junior year. I was in the hospital for reconstructive surgery on my face during what would have been my senior year."

Worse than that, he had smashed her computer to bits.

The silence fell heavy in the car. There was more to the story, so much more. But the less Holt knew about her and her family, the better.

"Then what happened?"

"I changed my name. My face was already changed." She hiccupped and gave a shaky laugh. Her calm façade was starting to break. "And I ran. I was lucky to get away. I ended up here."

Joely could feel Holt's judgement in the thickly charged silence between them.

"Did you press charges?"

"One of his brothers is a state cop and the other is a lawyer."

Holt's lips tightened. "He violated the restraining order and put you in the hospital. And now he's a state senator."

"Yes, but he lost the election that year." A hysterical giggle escaped her, and she clamped a hand over her mouth.

Holt pulled into the beach parking lot. It took everything in her not to bolt as soon as he unlocked the car doors. She forced herself to climb out of the car with as much grace and dignity that she could muster. He took the boards down from the roof of his car.

"Let me get your back, otherwise you're going to be a lobster." He reached in and grabbed the suntan lotion.

She braced herself for his touch, holding her breath. He smoothed the lotion over her shoulders first. His big hands were

24

warm and strong. She closed her eyes. It had been a long time since someone touched her so gently. Even if his strokes down her back and the back of her legs were efficient rather than lover-like, it was nice to be touched.

"Thanks," she whispered as he capped the bottle and tossed it back into the car.

"*'A'ole pilikia.*"

She shivered. He was almost unbearably sexy when he spoke Hawaiian. She concentrated on carrying the surfboard to the water without tripping or making a fool out of herself. She almost swallowed her tongue when Holt shrugged out of his shirt and dropped his shorts. He was wearing a bathing suit underneath, but for a moment she almost had a heart attack.

"Aren't you going to put on sunscreen?"

"Never leave the house without it." He grinned at her.

Well, damn. She had wanted to return the favor. Nothing ever went right for her.

D.T. Fleming was almost deserted this time of the morning during the week. The lifeguards were hanging out in their booth, but aside from a few families spread out along the beach, they had the place generally to themselves.

Joely wished she didn't have to leave. She was going to miss the beach, and the ocean, and the absolute feeling of peace she felt when paddling out to the waves.

Today the waves were flat, but it didn't matter. What mattered was the feel of the sun on her back, and the quiet strength of the man beside her. If things had been different or if they had more time, maybe they could have had something more than a co-worker, grudging friendship. They didn't say anything until they were out far enough that they were away from everyone else.

"Thanks for this," she said, and she heard the longing in her voice. "I'm going to miss Maui."

"I need you tell me everything," Holt said. He was sitting astride his board, his leg close enough to touch hers. She wanted to smooth her hand over the fine hairs of his leg and muscled thigh. Holt would always be forbidden fruit for her. He was too sharp to lie to, and he wasn't the type of man who would accept anything but the complete truth in a relationship. She couldn't give him that. The secrets she kept weren't only her own.

Timothy ruined everything. First by being a dirty politician, but mostly because he considered her to be a loose end. Maybe if she told him she was content being a missing person, he'd go back to Minnesota and forget about her.

And maybe it would snow on the beach today.

"It doesn't matter," she said.

"It does to me. It does to your friends."

Joely blinked back tears. "You can't help me. You don't know what he's like. He's ruthless."

"You've met my uncle, right?"

She was surprised she could still laugh, and was startled by the chuckle that escaped her. His uncle, Tetsuo, was rumored to be the *oyabun* of the local Yakuza clan. "Okay, point taken. The thing is if Timothy knows I'm at Palekaiko, he'll wait until I'm vulnerable. Then, he'll knock me out, and take me back to Minnesota. If he doesn't kill me out right, he'll keep me there until I escape. And before you tell me I'm being dramatic, he's done it before."

"That's kidnapping, a federal crime, especially if he takes you across state lines."

"If he's caught. If anyone believes me. And only if I escape this time. Like I said, he just might kill me."

26

She was fascinated by the muscle that worked in his jaw. Joely wanted to stroke his cheek and tell him not to worry. She'd get away from him again.

"Why does he want to kill you?"

And here was where things got tricky. She couldn't tell him the real reason, not without risking that he would turn her over to the police—or worse leave her all alone out on D.T. Fleming Beach. She'd be a sitting duck. "He didn't like that I filed for divorce. I embarrassed him." It wasn't even a lie. It just wasn't the whole truth.

Holt seemed to accept her explanation and that made her feel worse. She would have liked to tell him that her father and his uncle would have gotten along famously, but she knew that he wasn't close to Tetsuo and hated that he wasn't a legitimate business man.

"You need to go to the police. His brothers can't help him here."

She wasn't surprised that Holt recommended the police. In his world, the police were the good guys. Except for the ones who were owned by his uncle, or could be bought with Timothy's money.

"And tell them what?" She watched as the boogie boarders rode the small waves back to the beach. Paddling out farther, she just wanted to keep going. Let the ocean take her before her ex could. "He's done nothing wrong…yet. And by the time he does, it will be too late."

"What if we all sit down with him?" Holt paddled out so he was next to her again. "You'll be surrounded by your friends. We'll make sure you're never alone until he leaves."

That wouldn't work. If Timothy was backed into a corner, he'd start singing like a canary and paint her the villain. Joely didn't think she could take it if her friends looked at her differently after he spread his poison. And Holt was so straitlaced, he might insist on calling the police anyway—to arrest her. She was no angel. She had made a lot of mistakes that she was running from as well.

"He won't take no for an answer." Again not a lie, just not the complete truth. "That's why he's here after all these years. I will only be able to sleep at night if I'm a hundred percent sure Timothy has no idea where I am. So, I've got to leave this new life I built for myself and start over somewhere else. Maybe even change my name again."

"Maybe not," Holt said, his eyes lost in thought.

"What do you mean?" She pulled her feet on the board and wrapped her arms around her knees.

"He's here on vacation. Amelia checked his reservation. Two weeks and then he flies back to Minnesota."

"This was no chance meeting. He knew I was here." She hated that her voice shook.

"He saw a picture of you on somebody's social media page in your uniform. But he doesn't know that you're still here."

"I'm so fucked," Joely groaned, pressing her forehead to her knees. Of course, a wave smacked her off her board when she wasn't looking. She lost her hat and her sunglasses, but at least her bikini was still on—barely. As she adjusted her wardrobe malfunction under water, she looked up at the ankle leash holding her to the board and Holt's strong legs dangling from his board.

It was so peaceful and quiet, she wished she had the time to have taken a deeper breath. She'd like to stay down here forever. Too bad she wasn't a mermaid. Swimming up to the surface, she steadied herself on the surf board.

"For my next trick," she said, clambering back on the board. This time, she straddled it like Holt did for better balance. "I'd pull a rabbit out of my hat, if I still had one."

Holt wordlessly handed her back her hat.

"Thanks," she said.

"Be right back," he said, unclipping his leash then diving into the water.

Joely put her foot on his board so it wouldn't float away. Smoothing her hair back, she put it into a ponytail and wrung out her hat before jamming it on her head. A few minutes later Holt came up for air, but before she could ask him what he was doing, he dove underwater again.

Having grown up on Maui, Holt could hold his breath for a long time. He and the other guys took her out fishing one time. They didn't tell her until she was on the boat that they weren't going to use poles. They went spear fishing and she was the only one who had a snorkel and vest on. The other guys didn't need it.

This time when Holt came back up, he was holding her sunglasses.

"You didn't have to do that," Joely said, shocked. "But thank you."

"You're welcome. I think I know a way out of this. But I've got to make a few phone calls first. Let's go out for lunch."

She shook her head. "I can't risk Timothy seeing me."

"He's snorkeling in Molokini today."

Joely stared at him like he had two heads. "Timothy? Snorkeling?"

"I told you. He's on vacation first. He's not really expecting to find you. He's chasing a long shot. Once he checks things out, and you're not here, he'll go home."

Placing a hand over her heart that just started beating hard in her chest, she stared out into the waves. Could it be true? "So, you think that I can lay low in a hotel for two weeks and then everything will go back to normal?" That would play hell with her savings, but it would be completely worth it. She squinted at Holt. "Do you think Amelia will hold my job?"

"I can pretty much guarantee it. But I've got a better idea than a hotel. Come on Freckles, let me take you to lunch."

She would not blush. She would not blush. But his evil chuckle told her that her face was as red as her hair.

Chapter Four

Holt called his uncle when Joely went into the changing room to put her maid uniform back on. None of the restaurants he wanted to take her to would allow her inside wearing the two scraps of fabric she called a bikini. It was all he could do not to swim her out of lifeguard's view and see how strong those string ties really were.

"*Aloha* nephew," Tetsuo Hojo said. "I wasn't expecting to hear from you. Is Michael all right?"

Holt frowned. He hadn't heard from his brother in a few weeks. "I guess so. I haven't talked to him."

"Your mother wanted you to keep an eye on him."

Holt bristled at his uncle's chiding tone. "He's an adult. He can live his own life." After the long silence that followed, Holt sighed. "I will check up on him."

"*Mahalo*. Now what can I do for you?"

"I need to go Upcountry for two weeks. Is there room at the ranch for me and a friend?"

"Of course."

Holt had a feeling that he shocked his uncle, but before he could end the call, Tetsuo rallied.

"What about your job at the resort? Did they fire you?"

He didn't have to sound so giddy about it.

"No. I'm taking vacation."

"With a friend?" Tetsuo asked. "Is this a female friend?"

31

Holt groaned inwardly. He couldn't lie, yet if this got back to his mother she would get the wrong idea and start knitting booties for her expected grandchildren. "Yes," he said shortly, hoping that would be the end of the conversation.

He should have known better.

"Do I know her?"

"No, she works at the resort."

"Is it the red headed maid?" his uncle asked.

"How did you …?"

"I have eyes and ears everywhere, Holt. Yes, you two can stay at the ranch. But I will need you to help out while you're there. It will have to be a working vacation for you both."

His uncle could hire anyone he wanted for the ranch, so Holt doubted that was the case. He knew Tetsuo was just trying to get him back into the *paniolo* life in hopes that he'd quit Palekaiko and come back and work for him.

Still, it was worth it. Makawao was far away from the Palekaiko Beach Resort, and the ranch was secluded enough that a tourist would never find it.

"Of course," Holt agreed. "Whatever you need."

"When are you planning to take your vacation?"

"I'm driving up there after lunch today."

"That was a quick decision. What if I had said no?" Tetsuo asked, thoughtfully.

"I would have gone to the big island," Holt said. It was even true. He and Joely could easily hide in the city in places no tourist would ever go. But the ranch was nicer, and a part of him wanted her to see his boyhood home.

Tetsuo grunted, and Holt knew he had aroused his suspicions, but there was nothing he could do about it now. He just had to hope that he wasn't curious enough to come out to the ranch and investigate.

The next call was to his other boss, Dude's brother, Marcus in California where he gave him the whole story. Marcus said he'd get in contact with Amelia and see if they could dig up anything to leverage against the senator, if things got ugly. And he gave both Holt and Joely the two weeks off with pay.

There was something missing from Joely's story, though. The same niggling feeling that Holt had always had around her. She was hiding something else. He would bet money on it. He almost asked Marcus to do a background check on Annie Andrews, but he didn't want to break Joely's trust. Not yet. Holt had plenty of time to find out all her secrets once they were on the ranch.

Joely walked out of the changing room in her maid's uniform, but she was back to looking frightened.

"It's all right," he said as he secured the surf boards back to the roof of his car. "I've got the perfect solution."

"I'm listening." Joely crossed her arms in front of her chest.

Her body language told him she was protecting herself from something.

"I'll tell you over lunch."

She rolled her eyes at him. "You can be such a drama queen."

"I don't think anyone has ever accused me of that."

"That's because they're afraid of you," she said, climbing into the car.

"Do you want to swing by Palekaiko and pack some things?" he asked.

"Can we confirm he's at Molokini?"

Holt called Amelia. "Is our Senator friend on the boat?"

"Yup. He'll be back around four. I've told everyone that Joely does not want this guy to know where she is. She doesn't, right?"

"Affirmative." He smiled encouragingly at Joely.

"Okay, then we'll keep the faith."

"Thanks." Holt hung up. Then realized he should have asked Joely if she wanted to talk with Amelia. "Sorry," he said. "I didn't think. Do you want to call her back?"

Joely shook her head. "I'll do it later. Why am I packing a bag?"

"I've got a place for you to stay for two weeks or until your ex leaves."

"How much?"

"Free."

Cocking her head at him, she looked at him suspiciously. "Where?"

"You're not going to wait for lunch, are you?"

"Hell no."

"My family has a ranch up country in Makawao. We can stay there for two weeks and once your ex leaves, you can go back to your life."

"We?"

It figured that she would focus in on that. "It's a working ranch. There will be *paniolos* and ranch hands. You're going to have to pitch in."

"I don't know the first thing about cows or horses."

"Don't worry. I'll teach you."

"And your family is okay with me hiding out there?"

"I told them it was just a vacation, to get away from the tourists. I figured the less they know the better."

Joely nodded. "Yes. Definitely." She sighed and wrung her hands. "I think that could work, if he actually does leave at the end of the two weeks."

"Great." Holt was satisfied. Problem presented. Problem solved. It only proved that order can be brought out of chaos with careful thought and planning.

He could see Joely's mood brightening and relaxing as they got closer to the resort.

"And the cherry on the cake is, Marcus is going to give you these two weeks with pay."

Her smile was beautiful and lit something inside him. He had to force his eyes back to the road.

"Holt, I don't know what to say. Thank you. This has been hanging over me for a long time. If he stops looking for me here, then I can be safe." She put her hand on his arm and squeezed.

The innocent touch shouldn't have affected him as it did. The other part of being a white knight in shining armor was it was bad form to seduce the princess. After the rescue, however...

It had been five years, Holt could wait another two weeks.

She was laughing at the chickens running away from his car when he parked in the Palekaiko garage. "Better run chickies otherwise you're going to be lunch."

When they got out of the car, she launched herself at him, hugging him tight. It was only natural that he returned the hug.

"Thank you, Holt." Her voice was muffled against his shirt and he realized that he didn't want her gratitude. For the first time in his life, he didn't want to be the white knight. He wanted to be the dragon, because the dragon got to ravage the princess.

She fit into his arms like she belonged there. Her silky hair was curling out of her ponytail and smelled like the ocean, crisp and pure. It was second nature to brush his lips against her temple. She was warm and sweet, her soft curves resting against him trustingly. Would she run away if she knew that he'd like nothing more than to lay her back on the hood of his car and kiss her senseless?

Cupping her cheek, he tilted her face up to his. Her green eyes were dazed and slightly unfocused. Holt dragged his thumb over her lower lip. When she parted them, he swooped in with a groan and covered her mouth with his.

Holt meant it to be an innocent kiss, a quick brush that promised more later, when it would be more ethical to pursue something deeper. The moment Joely went up on her tip toes to deepen the kiss, all his good intentions went south—along with all his blood to his cock.

Her fingers clutched on his bicep as he slanted his mouth across hers. Holt cupped her ass and brought her hard against him. Joely wrapped her arms around his neck and allowed her entire body to rest against his.

Holt bit back a groan at the roar of desire that flooded through him when she tried to wiggle closer. The sound of car doors slamming broke them apart, and Holt didn't know if he should apologize or throw her over his shoulder and carry her off to his apartment.

Her naughty grin almost made his mind up, but then she turned around and walked toward the lobby and he was distracted by the sweet sway of her ass. Clicking the lock on his car, he pocketed the keys and followed her.

It was because he had his eyes on her ass that he didn't see Timothy until Joely froze dead in her tracks. Time slowed down when Timothy turned and recognized her.

"Annie!"

Joely turned and sprinted past Holt. He had recovered enough wits to step in front of the senator.

"Get out of my way," Timothy snarled, trying to physically move Holt. Good luck with that.

"She doesn't want to see you," Holt said.

"You lied to me before. Why should I believe you now?" He tried to sidestep past Holt, but Holt was too quick for him.

"You lied as well. About a lot of things. Consider me her new restraining order."

"You don't understand. She's not who you think she is."

A large roar echoed across the parking lot behind them as a big motorcycle engine started up. Holt was hoping the senator would push by him or put his hands on him. Anything to justify Holt decking him. But after sidestep dancing for a few more seconds, the motorcycle ripped by them both.

"She's getting away," Timothy said, outraged.

Sure enough, Joely was tearing out of the parking lot on Dude's Harley going way too fast for the curves. Her uniform skirt was hiked up high and her bare thigh nearly kissed the ground as she took the first curve low and fast.

Makoa shook his head. "So much for the *wilwil*."

"Did she just steal a motorcycle?" Timothy said. "Call the cops."

"It's borrowed," Amelia said, quickly.

"I need a taxi." Timothy stepped into the street and started waving his hands around.

Hani and Kai joined them looking out at the disappearing dot that was Joely on Dude's bike.

"She's gone," Hani said.

Kai nodded. "Gonna take something faster than a taxi to catch her."

"We'll just see about that." Timothy stormed back into the resort.

Chapter Five

Joely opened the bike up when she hit highway thirty and let all her attention focus on not crashing Dude's motorcycle. She was proud of herself that she still remembered how to hot wire a bike. As highway thirty turned into Honoapiilani highway, she eased off the throttle. Where the hell was she going to go? She was on an island.

She pulled into her bank and closed the account, taking the cash in hundreds and smaller bills. It was a depressingly short stack. She stuffed the envelope in Dude's saddle bag and got back on the bike. It was tempting to take a ride all the way up to Hana and see if she could go live off the grid for a while.

She stopped at Walmart in Kahului for a change of clothes so she wouldn't stand out like a sore thumb in flip flops and her maid's uniform. Stuffing everything into the backpack she also bought, she was ready to make her escape. Since she was so close to the airport, Joely considered parking the bike in short term parking and be on the next flight out.

"That's the first place they'd look," she decided. She didn't want to keep running, looking over her shoulder. Timothy could pull a few strings, or his brother could and find out which flight she took out. They could even have someone waiting for her at her arrival gate, where ever that happened to be. No, she had to play this smart for now. Tightening the hoodie she bought at Walmart, so that her head was covered, she headed back towards Lahaina.

Dressed now in jeans, sneakers and the black hoodie that hid her hair and face, the only one who'd possibly be able to recognize her from the opposite side of the road was Dude because she couldn't disguise the bike. It was all flashy chrome and tricked out. Amelia should have known Dude wasn't a beach bum when she saw the bike. Joely shook her head. She pegged Dude as a rich boy slacker almost immediately. He was a good guy, though. And she was glad he and Amelia were together.

As she entered Olowalu, she decided to stop at Leoda's Kitchen and Pie shop. Dude was going to be pissed about the bike. Maybe if she bought him a macadamia nut chocolate pie, he might not mind that she borrowed it. She could leave the bike here with a note at the counter for him. She just needed to figure out where the heck she was going.

After placing her order for a hand-held carnita pie, pineapple coleslaw, and some lemonade, she took a seat in the back of the busy restaurant. She'd be able to see people coming and going, but even if Timothy was tracking her down he probably wouldn't stop here for some *ono grindz*. It wasn't classy enough for him. To her, though, it was paradise. She was going to miss every single thing about this island, from the food, to the people, to the ocean.

Part of her, the long-suppressed part of her, whispered, "Killing Timothy is the only way to be able to stay here safely."

Joely shook her head fiercely. That was her sister talking. Katie was currently doing time for murder.

Another ghost from her past whispered from pushed aside memories. "Call your sister. She'll get you new papers."

That was her father talking. But he wasn't talking about Katie, he was talking about her other sister.

The last time she spoke to Sammy was a little over five years ago. Sammy was a forger, apprenticed to their uncle when she was old enough to write. She was the one who had gotten Joely her new identity, and helped her escape from the hospital under everyone's noses. Joely might be able to find her. She opened up the backpack and saw the new laptop she purchased at Walmart. Her fingers itched to do it.

No.

She promised herself never to contact her family again. It would be like falling into quicksand. One little thing would spiral into another until the next thing she knew she would be hacking databases, cracking safes, or running cons again. She didn't even know why she bought the laptop. It was too much temptation. She didn't even have one in her room at Palekaiko. A part of her wondered if she lost her skills.

"Here ya go sistah," the waitress said, sliding her food over to her.

"Thanks," she said, glad for the tart, cold lemonade to ground her into the present. She was no longer in that life. Her family wasn't the solution. They were the problem. If her father knew she was on the run again, he'd offer to help.

If she helped him back.

She zipped up the backpack, covering up the temptation of the laptop.

She wondered if her parents were still alive. The last she heard they were down in Australia whale hunting. Only not the type of whales you saw in the ocean. The types with more money than brains. It occurred to her that if her parents knew she was best friends with the wives of two millionaires, they would be island bound. She wouldn't let her parents ruin her life like they did her sisters'.

Joely hadn't realized how hungry she was until she got a whiff of the savory pie. She inhaled her lunch and leaned back in her chair. She still didn't know what she was going to do.

Deciding to call Amelia, she walked outside. Tying the hoodie around her waist, she darted around the building so she couldn't be seen from the road.

It went to voice mail.

"Well, shit." Joely thumped her foot against the wall.

Her phone began ringing almost immediately. It was Holt.

"I thought Timothy was in Molokini," she accused, but she was too tired to put any heat in it.

"He got seasick and made the boat turn around."

Joely groaned. "I need you and Dude to come pick up his bike."

"Where are you?"

"Don't worry about me. Tell Dude there's a pie waiting for him at Leoda's."

"Don't move. We'll be right there. You're coming to Makawao with me.

Chapter Six

Holt pulled into Leona's. Dude made a beeline to his bike. While he checked it out, Holt strode through the restaurant, scanning for Joely.

He didn't see her. Frustrated, he turned back to the parking lot and saw Dude talking to a figure in a black hoodie. That had better fucking be her.

As he walked up, some of the tension left his back when he recognized her voice.

"Bring it into the shop. The transmission hitched when I shifted into fifth gear."

"Are you sure you didn't lug the motor? Or broke something when you hotwired it?"

Dude was so pissed, he forgot he was supposed to be a stoner idiot instead of a billionaire stock broker hiding out from responsibilities.

"Positive," Joely said, hands on her hips. "I was at 3,000 RPM doing 75mph before I shifted into fifth. It wasn't redlining when I got it up to 90."

"I don't want to hear anything else. La la la, I'm not listening to you." Dude stuck his fingers in his ears.

She took one hand and yanked it down. "I'm sorry I borrowed your bike without asking."

Dude shrugged. "I heard it was a pretty epic escape."

Making a face, Joely said, "Yeah, it would have been if my entire life wasn't upset by it."

"Don't worry, *wahine*. We'll figure something out." He tried to ruffle her hair under the hoodie, but she smacked his hand away.

Holt smirked.

"There's a pie with your name on it inside." She pointed.

"Sweet." Dude grinned.

And with that, all was forgiven. Dude didn't hold a grudge and he had been just as worried as the rest of them when Amelia broke the news to him that Joely "borrowed" his pride and joy.

Dude had wanted to kick Timothy out on his well-padded ass, but Holt had convinced him to let him stay in order to keep a better eye on him. They agreed to tell Joely's ex that Holt and Joely had been fired. Because if Timothy thought that they were in the wind, hopefully he'd leave and never come back.

Joely grabbed Dude in for a quick hug. "Tell Amelia I'll call her."

"Shoots." Dude nodded. "We'll see you in a few weeks."

Giving him a tight-lipped nod, she turned to Holt and he didn't quite recognize the woman in front of him. Yeah, it was Joely. And yet, it was also Annie, and she looked tough and wary. She reminded him of a feral cat that had the intelligence to know she couldn't make it out in the woods without help, yet wasn't sure she could trust being domesticated.

"I packed you a bag," Holt said.

"Where's Timothy?" She fiddled at the string tie of her hoodie, but followed him to his car.

After they got in, she slumped down in the seat and locked her door.

"Amelia and Makoa were keeping him occupied while I got Dude and your things."

"He'll never leave now. He'll have people watching the airports. I'll have to take a boat to the big island and try to lose his trackers. Except now he's got my new name and information. I'm not sure how long I'll be able to stay hidden."

"Just give me two weeks. Same plan."

"Same plan?" Joely straightened up in her seat and her hoodie fell off. Her hair scattered over her face and shoulders. She brushed it back in aggravation. "He's not going to do touristy things. He's coming for me."

"He won't find you. And if he does, he can't get to you on the ranch."

"I can't stay there forever."

Holt wondered if she could. She could be a housekeeper there. Her ex would have to get through ten pretty ornery cowboys to get to her. "Let's just try it for two weeks."

"He won't leave. Not without me."

"He'll have to see reason with Amelia and Makoa working on him, and the fact that you ran away from him. They're going to tell him that you and I got fired and ran away together."

Joely sighed. "He'll tell lies about me. He'll make you all doubt me. You don't understand how charismatic he can be."

"Maybe not, but I know Makoa and Amelia. You're Makoa's friend. He'll believe you over any haole. You're Amelia's friend too. She'll make Timothy wish he had never been born if he starts on you. Don't forget Micheala. She can charge him with slander."

Joely gave a half smile, and he thought that was better than nothing. "I guess," she said, grudgingly. She looked up at him through her lashes. "What about you?"

"Me?"

45

"What if he tells his lies to you? Who would you believe?"

"I would believe you."

She shook her head. "He's damned convincing, and you're naturally suspicious."

"I'd hear your side of the story before I did anything rash. Of course, it would help if I knew your story to begin with."

"I told you my story," she said hotly, maybe a little desperately.

"Not everything."

She flinched.

"You can tell me when you're ready, but I think you should tell me sooner rather than later."

Joely didn't say anything else and while they drove she stared out the window. Holt wished he could get a better read on her.

As they entered old town Makawao, the traffic was at a standstill. It was a busy day with tourists checking out the shops and galleries. There was a line down the block outside of T Komoda Bakery. Holt glanced at the clock. He was surprised there was anything left this late in the afternoon, usually they were sold out by eleven.

"Have you ever been Upcountry before?" he asked. He didn't know much about Joely's personal life. She never seemed to leave the Palekaiko resort, unless she was with one of the staff.

"Yeah, briefly. We went up to the Haleakala for a picnic one night." She grinned. "Makoa thought he should make an offering to the island spirits so the volcano wouldn't erupt for another nine hundred years."

"I appreciate his efforts," Holt said. Makoa was a gentle giant. He wasn't the sharpest knife in the drawer, but he had a good heart.

46

"He wasted a good bottle of rum, pouring it into the ground."

"I'm sure there was enough rum for everyone, including the spirits. Was it just you two?" Holt noticed that out of all the other staff members, she spent a lot of time with the hulking bell boy.

"No, Hani and Theresa were there too. And a few of their family. It was nice of them to invite me."

"I wasn't invited."

"You were probably off saving the world from evil or something," she said lightly.

"Is that how you see me? A superhero?" There were worse things.

"Boy Scout," she said.

His ego deflated like a balloon, complete with the raspberry sound of air escaping. "I'm no boy. Haven't been for a long time."

Unzipping her hoodie, she shrugged it off. Holt was glad. The black color made her look sad. "Well, man scout sounds ridiculous. You're so straight and narrow, I bet you starch your Hawaiian shirt so it doesn't wrinkle."

"In this heat?" He arched an eyebrow at her.

"You know what I mean."

"You're calling me a tight ass."

"I never said those words," she protested. Then chuckled. "But if the shoe fits, feel free to lace them up."

"If you had an uncle like mine, you'd understand why following rules and obeying the law is so important to me."

The soft amusement fled from her face and he got another zing in his intuition. Maybe she did have someone like his uncle in her

47

past. He cleared his throat and said, "Not that Tetsuo has been anything but generous and kind to me and my brother."

"What's Mike up to anyways? I haven't seen him since he left the resort," she asked.

"That's a good question," Holt said, scanning the streets as if he might see his brother. He might. The family ranch wasn't too much farther away. "I don't worry too much about him. Mike had an idea to "live off the grid" a few years ago, and a couple of the paniolos nearly ran over him and his yurt with their ATVs."

"ATVs? Isn't that cheating?"

Laughing, Holt shook his head. "They use the horses for the work close to the ranch, but it's more efficient to use the all-terrain vehicles when hunting down a wandering calf."

"Still seems like cheating. So, what did they do to Mike when they found him?"

"Kicked him out of the pasture. Made him go back to the ranch house. My uncle dealt with him. Got him a job in Hana."

"What was he using for food? Did he go diving for fish?"

Holt shook his head. "Too far away. I think he was living off ramen noodles and the money my mother would send him."

"Where's she?"

"Kyoto. She had enough of the cowboy life and the resort life. She works in a glass and metal cube farm in the business district." Holt shuddered. He had trouble breathing just thinking about it.

"What does she do there?"

"She works for an insurance company processing claims. It's a good job. She loves it. Loves being in the city." Loves being out from her brother's thumb, and divorced from her husband. He didn't want to talk about his family anymore. It always made him edgy and restless.

Holt pointed down a road. "There's a block party next Friday. They close off the street. We should go, if you like."

She blushed. "Are you asking me out on a date?"

"That depends."

"On what?"

"Would you be more comfortable if we just went as friends?"

"I don't know," she said.

It wasn't a resounding yes, but it sounded encouraging.

A few miles later he made the turn off to the Hojo ranch. So many feelings bounced around inside him and he clenched his jaw to keep them from doing damage. They were only memories and they didn't have the power to hurt him anymore.

"You all right?" Joely asked, laying a hand on his arm.

"It's weird being back after all these years. I was born here."

"What's a born cowboy like you doing security on a beach resort then?"

It hurt being back. Holt acknowledged that. The green rolling hills called to him and the red gusts of dirt that covered his car were familiar as a pair of faded jeans.

He snorted. "I'm going to need a few beers before we get into that story."

"We should have stopped to get some," she said.

"You don't know paniolos very well. Beer is the last thing we'll be missing."

The farmhouse was just coming into view in the distance. For a moment, time reversed and he could see himself and Mike running down the path. He had been ten and Mike had been five. They hadn't wanted to leave the farm and go live on the beach where there weren't any horses. But the ranch hands caught them and threw them screaming into their father's beat up truck.

"Holy shit, Holt. When you said you're taking me to a ranch, I didn't picture anything so huge."

Joely's exclamation broke him out of his thoughts. He wasn't ten anymore. He made his life away from the horses and cattle on the beach. This was just a vacation.

"It's been in my mother's family for decades." Holt pointed up to the window on the far left of the farmhouse. "That used to be me and Mike's bedroom."

He parked next to the garage.

Joely got out and gaped. "I could spend forever looking at the scenery. Haleakala is gorgeous."

Holt smiled at the enormous dormant volcano. "Maybe we can take a bike ride up there this week?"

Her face lit up. "You have a motorcycle?"

"Wilwil," Holt said sheepishly.

"Nah, that's way too much like work." She giggled. "Hiking maybe. As long as there's a stocked picnic basket afterwards."

"I think I can arrange that."

"So, that's two dates." She held up two fingers.

"We are on vacation." He reminded her with a wink, watching as she twirled around in a circle.

"I can't believe how gorgeous this place is. It goes on forever."

"Four thousand acres."

Joely did a double take. "You're kidding, right? You're rich."

50

"My uncle is rich. I work security for the Palekaiko Beach Resort." Holt didn't want anything to do with how Tetsuo made money to keep the ranch in the black. His father tried by the sweat of his brows and nearly bankrupted it.

"You should tell Amelia about this. She'd go crazy setting up horseback riding tours."

"She'd go crazy working with Tetsuo." Holt said. "Do you ride?"

"I did the touristy meanderings on an old nag when I first got here. Almost got dumped into the ocean."

"You won't have to worry about that here. Hookipa is the closest beach. We can go surfing too."

"Date number three. This is getting serious," she joked.

Holt hoped so. "Come on, I'll give you the grand tour."

Chapter Seven

Joely gaped at her surroundings. Everything here was so vast. She could see for miles. The cows on the hills looked like little toys. Everything was shades of green and blue in the distance. Up close, it was shades of red and brown. Dust, leather, wood. It felt comforting, like home. She could see for miles. She would be able to see Timothy coming.

Holt got her bag out of the trunk and motioned her to follow him up to the ranch house.

And he'd have to get through Holt, too.

Fat chance.

She'd seen Holt back down a bunch of vicious surfers defending their turf. Timothy didn't stand a chance. Admiring Holt's wide back as she followed him inside, Joely felt some of the anxiety that had been suffocating her, ease away.

Shopping, hiking, surfing and the possibility of a bit of romance with her hunky crush? This was turning out to be the best vacation of her life—if only she could forget about her ex-husband.

"Auntie?" Holt called out as he opened the screen door and nodded for Joely to go ahead of him.

The ranch house was rustic, with woven tapestry rugs and driftwood on the walls. But it had modern touches here and there. The large overhead fan circled its blades in a fast pace overhead. It was a refreshing breeze from the heat of the afternoon. Joely recognized a few paintings from local artists that had been featured at Palekaiko during one of Amelia's events.

Bustling out of one of the rooms came a beautiful woman who launched herself into Holt's arms.

Awkward.

Joely hadn't even considered that Holt might have a girlfriend. But no, the woman kissed him on both cheeks and hugged him more maternally than a lover would.

"You're home. You're home. You're finally home," she said, her big brown eyes filling with tears.

Holt tried to extricate himself from her embrace. "It's just for a visit, Kala. Two weeks."

"After two weeks, you won't want to go back to working with those haoles."

Clearing his throat, Holt side stepped Kala and stood next to Joely. "I'm here with my friend. Joely, this is my Aunt Kala."

Blinking, Joely shook the woman's hand. She really was his aunt. She had assumed Holt was using the respectful title of Auntie.

"It's nice to meet you," Kala said. "Tetsuo said you work with Holt."

"Yes." Joely tried to take her hand back, but Kala held on tight.

Originally Joely had thought Kala was their age, but looking into her flawless face she could see that she was closer to double that. Her gaze was stern and assessing. Joely could feel herself starting to sweat, even with the breeze that kicked up from the ceiling fans.

"I'm happy to welcome you to my home."

Casting a panicked look at Holt, Joely said, "You and Tetsuo live here?"

"When we choose. He's sorry he's not here to greet you, himself, but he had important business. He should be here for dinner."

"Dinner?" she squeaked. She hadn't planned on dining with the Japanese mob.

"Uncle Tetsuo didn't mention he would be here," Holt said.

Kala shrugged one shoulder. "He doesn't tell me many things either. Come, let me show you to your rooms."

To Joely's relief, Kala released her and led them up a grand staircase that was more fitting to a mansion than a farm house.

"This is your room," she said, opening a heavy wooden door.

The doors of the balcony had been opened and the scent of lavender and eucalyptus floated around the room. A fresh bouquet of both was on the nightstand near an enormous canopy bed.

"It's lovely," Joely said, walking in. The hardwood floor was accented by a turquoise rug that reminded her of the ocean.

Holt tossed her bags on the bed, and she winced because of the laptop. But the fluffy blue comforter absorbed the impact.

"The bathroom is down the hall. Come, let me show you."

With a quick look at Holt, who rolled his eyes, she followed Kala. The bathroom was as big as her entire apartment at the Palekaiko beach resort. There was a large claw footed tub underneath a floor-to-ceiling window. Joely couldn't help but wonder if the paniolos could get an eyeful or if it was too far up. There was also a shower stall that easily could fit a few horses inside.

"Holt will be staying in his room on the third floor," Kala remarked. "We don't have any other guests, so you should have this all to yourself."

"Sounds wonderful," she said, amused by Holt's frown.

"I'll leave you to get settled in. Dinner is at six. Dress casual."

That was good because she hadn't brought anything formal.

"Um, is there Wi-Fi?" Joely asked. It didn't mean she was going to use it, but it was good to know.

Kala frowned. "Yes, but I don't know the password."

"I do," Holt said. "It's a long one. I'll text it to you."

Waving her hand, Kala said, "Too much technology. Come, Holt, wait until you see what I've done to you and Mikey's room."

"Mikey?" Joely mouthed.

Holt waved his phone at her. "Call me, if you need anything."

"I'll be fine. Kala, thank you so much for letting me stay here."

"Of course," she said. "You're the first girl Holt has ever brought home."

"Really?" Joely said, smiling wide at Holt's mortified expression.

"Auntie, is there anything to eat? I'm a little hungry," he said.

"Of course, there is. I have some saimin left over from lunch and some poke. Joely, would you care to join us?

"It sounds delicious, but I don't want to spoil my appetite for dinner. I think I'll just get settled, and take a rest."

Kala nodded in approval and walked away.

"If you don't hear from me in a half hour, call in the cavalry," Holt said, leaning in to mutter in her ear.

Shivers tickled over her from his breath and she bit her lip. "I wouldn't even know who to call."

"Wish me luck, then."

She gave him the shaka as Kala called out, "Holt? Where are you?"

"Be right there, Auntie." He walked Joely back to her room. "I'm sorry about this. I thought we'd have the place to ourselves. She's usually at her condo in Wailea."

"Hey, it's okay. You guys are doing me a big favor. I just don't want to drag even more people into my drama with Timothy."

"It won't get to that. But even if it did, my money is on Aunt Kala. I'll see you later."

He brushed a quick kiss over her cheek and was gone before the gasp left her mouth. Rubbing where his lips touched, she went into her room and closed the door. Leaning against it, she nearly sagged to the floor.

She was safe here. She could sense it. She was truly off the grid here. And that had its pros and cons. But Joely was savvy enough to know that this was only temporary. If she wanted to go back to work at the Palekaiko Beach Resort, she had to make sure that Timothy didn't leave any spies to watch out for her. Unfortunately, there wasn't an easy way to do that. Her skills were rusty and she didn't have the latest and greatest equipment.

But she did know Timothy. Even if he had changed his passwords, she knew she could hack into to his email and voicemail.

Joely spent the next half hour setting up the laptop. When Holt texted her the Wi-Fi password, she thought long and hard about connecting to it. Did she really want to do this? It was a slippery slope. She wasn't a criminal anymore. She gave up that life when she gave up her identity as Annie Andrews.

It wasn't like she was going to sell any data that she found. She was just going to see who Timothy was talking to and what he was planning on doing.

Sighing, she logged onto the internet for the first time in five years.

56

It took her longer than she expected to get back into the swing of things. Digging out a notebook, she wrote down things she would need to buy at an electronics store. Or she could order it online if they would ship it to the ranch.

She cracked Timothy's password to his Gmail account in no time and as she scrolled through the past day and a half, she didn't see anything helpful. He hadn't changed his passwords on any of his social media, so she got in there and poked around too.

Bo-ring!

Still, he was dumb enough to post pictures of Lahaina, advertising to everyone that he wasn't in his Minnesota home at the moment. Hopefully, the thieves over there were paying attention. If they wanted to rob him, chances are they wouldn't run into anyone home.

Scrolling through them, she saw that he really was on vacation first and foremost. He wasn't letting a little thing like looking for his ex-wife stop him from sightseeing.

What she really needed was remote access to his computer. Joely could compose a phishing email, but there wasn't a good chance that he'd see it in time or even click on it. She nibbled on her lip. If she could access his laptop, she could install a key logger on his computer in addition to giving herself remote access.

All she had to do was sneak back into his room at Palekaiko and install some software. Heart pounding, she considered it. She cursed at herself. Like the last time she did that, it ended so well. Timothy caught her and beat the shit out of her, smashing her laptop across her face. Rubbing her jaw, Joely didn't feel afraid. She was angry.

It wasn't going to go down like that again. She'd be more careful. But how?

One of the pictures he had on his Facebook wall was near the Sunset restaurant, which was on the water in Lahaina. It was a nice place, but Timothy was cheap. He wouldn't have forked over the cash for a sit-down dinner when he could get something to go. Not on his dime anyway. Not when Palekaiko included dining room meals with most of their vacation packages.

That's it. That's how she'd get him away from the resort.

Setting her computer aside, she crept to the door and opened it. She could hear faint voices down the stairs, Holt's deep rumble and then feminine laughter. Closing the door, she took out her cell phone and dialed Sunset.

"Aloha," Joely said in a perky fake voice, when a woman answered the phone. "I'm Marjorie Pierson with Go Go Hawaii. We're a marketing group from the Big Island and we've chosen your restaurant to host one of our contest winners. I'd like to purchase a hundred-dollar gift certificate for him to use for Thursday night. Only good for Thursday, though, okay? That's when we have our publicity set up for."

The woman agreed and Joely gave her Timothy's name and where he was staying. Reluctantly, she pulled out her credit card and gave her the information. She kept her fingers crossed and hoped that they wouldn't verify the name on the card. Luck was with her when the charge went through.

When that was taken care of, she went online and quickly banged together a cheap website using stock photos and opened up an email account for Go Go Hawaii and the fictitious Marjorie Pierson. Then she drafted a congratulatory email, using details from Timothy's travel agent and the airline confirmations in order to make it look legitimate.

After she sent it, she masked her cell phone with a random Hawaiian phone number and labeled it Go Go Hawaii. That way if anyone called it or she called anyone it would show a different name and number than hers.

Now, it was just a matter of waiting to see if the fish would take the bait.

Just like old times.

If Timothy went to the restaurant, she'd have a good time frame to sneak into his room and gain total access to his computer and files. Joely could see who he was contacting and what he was planning. She could stay one step ahead of him. But more importantly, she would know whether or not she could stay safely on Maui. Or if she'd have to start all over with another identity.

Speaking of which, she should contact Sammy just in case. It took a while to put together passports, birth certificates and other paperwork to fool the government.

Joely sent out emails to the three accounts that she knew her sister checked. Then against her better judgement, she put a classified ad in under the roommates' section on Craig's List.

It was a risk. There was a good chance that her parents would see it and also contact her. But Joely was desperate, so she put in an ad designed by her family to contact each other when they were separated and possibly compromised. She felt like a criminal even using it.

"I'm not doing anything wrong." She glossed over hacking Timothy's computer. That was self-preservation. She remembered their family's code as if it had been five minutes instead of five years.

Alexandria – Luxury Living

Why Alexandria? After the library that was destroyed in ancient Egypt. It symbolized things had hit the fan. Luxury Living

59

was a reference to their grifting and the good life they were all supposed to have.

Joely shook her head. One sister in jail. One on the run, and one working outside of the law. Yeah, this was the life.

$1198.50

That one was easy. The rent was who needed assistance. In this case, Joely used her real name Annie. A was the first letter of the alphabet. N was the nineteenth. You only counted the first N otherwise the number would be too long. I was the eighth letter of the alphabet and E was the fifth. So, *Annie* spelled out that way was *11985*.

That was her code number. Her sisters and parents had their own code based on the letters in their first names as well.

1 bedroom

She was alone.

1 bath

She was in priority one hot water, meaning she was in trouble and needed assistance immediately.

Fireplace

She was burned, meaning her identity was compromised.

Balcony

People were watching her.

Parking

But she was safe for the moment.

Near Public Transportation

She needed an exit strategy that included long distance travel.

The best way to reach her was online.

Holt knocked on the door and she almost tossed the laptop on the floor in surprise.

"Come in," she squeaked.

"You ready for dinner?" He poked his head in and gave her a smile.

Guilt flooded over her. She shouldn't be here. She was putting him and his family at risk. Not just from Timothy, but if her parents answered that ad there would be no stopping them from trying to steal from her friends. Joely was better off just leaving.

"Sure. Just give me a second."

"You got it." He closed the door behind him.

She read the ad over once more and pressed the button to make it live. There was no turning back now. She'd get a response within a day, maybe even sooner.

Joely hoped it would be Sammy.

Chapter Eight

As luck would have it, Tetsuo wasn't able to make it to dinner last night. Kala was ready to spit nails. Holt was glad he wasn't on the end of her temper today. Even still, he had plans to take Joely for a horseback ride today even though Tetsuo had wanted him to go right to work.

"Well, look at the city boy thinking he's a paniolo," Joe, the foreman, said coming into the barn.

"Is he wearing perfume?" Tony, one of the old timers, said from the door. "He smells purty."

"It's called a shower *lolo*. You should try it," Holt said, trying to hide his smile.

"You think the cattle are going to move from *Ushi* to *Buru* while you get your beauty sleep?" Joe snarled.

It took Holt a moment to realize his Uncle named the pastures *Cow* and *Bull* in Japanese. Which while accurate, wasn't very creative. When his mother was here, they were named after flowers. Holt supposed that the paniolos thought it was an improvement from moving the herd from Frangipani to Plumeria.

"I figured my friend and I would have a day or two to get situated. You don't want a greenhorn, and someone who hasn't stepped foot on this ranch in a few years, to hit the ground running without any orientation. We'd just get in your way."

Joe squinted at him and grunted. "Yeah, well don't think you're going to herd from the back of the pack. I want you up front rustling."

Holt found himself looking forward to it. Even though he had left the ranch when he was ten, he came back during the summers to work. At least, he did before the divorce. Then he had all to do to keep the resort running while his father drank the day away.

"I need some help with the fencing today too. Think you and your friend can patch up some barbed wire? Or are you afraid of getting your hands all cut up?"

"Holt?" Joely said, coming around the side of the barn.

Joe and Tony whipped off their hats. "Ma'am," Joe said.

Holt glared at him, wondering if they were being disrespectful, but a quick look at the two paniolos showed they were dazzled by Joely's smile and pretty face.

"Kala said you'd be out here." She hefted a backpack. "I've got lunch."

"Great, I'm just finishing up saddling the horses for our ride."

"This is your friend?" Tony laughed. "So much for getting any work done."

Joely crossed her arms over her chest. "I can pull my own weight."

"Yeah? What's that, ninety-eight pounds?" Tony asked.

Joely's face lit up. "I know you thought that was an insult, but not even close."

"I'm going to show her around the ranch today," Holt interrupted before Tony could think of a comeback. "We'll report for duty four a.m. tomorrow morning."

"Four?" Joely choked, then wiped her face clean of reaction when the two older paniolos glanced at her. "Four it is," she said, nodding.

"Well, I suppose you can muck out the stalls," Joe grumbled. "Forget about the barbed wire."

"Good to have you back, *keiki*," Tony said, and with a lingering look at Joely, followed Joe out of the barn.

"Why did he call you a child?"

Holt led the mare that Kala told him to give to Joely out of the stall. He had already saddled the horse for her. "He was more of a father to me than my own father. That was Tony, and the other one was Joe. He's the foreman. He's mostly all bark and no bite. Unless he finds you slacking off, and then he'll take a bite all right."

"I'll try to keep up." Joely petted the horse's neck.

"You don't have to get up at four o'clock with the rest of us."

"Why do you get up so early anyway?"

"The heat. The hotter it gets, the ornerier the cattle get. So, it's easier to feed and then move them while it's still cool out."

"You guys are doing me a huge favor. I can sacrifice a few hours of sleep, shovel shit or whatever else you want."

"If it was just me, they'd work me like a dog. With you here, we may just get off easy."

"Glad to be of service."

He walked the mare out to the pen. "Her name is Uma. Just hold on to her while I get Scout saddled."

Of course, he didn't have a horse of his own anymore. So, he picked out one of the spare work horses that had a little spunk in him.

"I thought we were going to take the ATVs," she said, sounding a bit nervous.

Holt glanced out, but Uma was behaving herself. "We can tomorrow. I figured I'd give you the authentic experience. Although we're a little late in the day for that."

64

"Sorry," she said.

"No worries." Holt dragged out a set of stairs and set them by Uma.

"Oh, thank God," Joely said. "I couldn't figure out how I was going to get up in the saddle without falling on my ass or twisting my ankle."

He helped her settle on top of the horse, and then slung himself up into his own saddle.

"Show off," she said, with a trace of admiration.

Grinning at her, he clicked his tongue and the two horses started moving.

"Hey, how did you do that?"

"These guys are very well trained. Just hold on to the reins and follow me. I figure we'll be out for a couple of hours, but if you get sore or need a break let me know."

Holt handed her a ball cap to put on her head. "It's going to get pretty windy." He adjusted his own.

They rode off in comfortable silence for a while. The afternoon was hot, but the quiet made up for it. A part of him missed the ocean breeze, but not the clamor of tourists or the busy bustle of the beach. It was peaceful out here, but he found that it was harder to escape his thoughts in all the silence.

"How many people work the farm?" Joely asked, startling him. He had almost forgotten she was there.

"About ten people give or take. There's about fifty cows, and not a lot of upkeep. But there's a lot of work keeping the pastures tended and the fences standing. When Kala and Tetsuo aren't here, Joe is the cook. There's the bunkhouse where they live." He pointed to a large building closer towards the barns.

"That's a bit further from the main house than I would have thought." Joely rode stiffly, but for a beginner she was doing all right in the saddle. He was glad to share all of this with her. He should have asked her out a long time ago instead of waiting for something so dire like this to get them together.

"Tetsuo doesn't like to mix with the paniolos. He hates them."

"Why?"

Yeah, why? Holt sighed. Great topic to begin the day with. "Because my father was one of them. And Tetsuo never quite forgave him for impregnating his sister outside of marriage."

"I'm sorry," she said. "You don't have to tell me this if you don't want to."

Holt shrugged. "It is what it is. There was a shotgun wedding and six months later, I came into this world. From what I gathered, Mel got his shit together and stopped drinking. He got promoted to foreman. Then Mike came along and it all went to hell."

Joely put a hand on his arm. "I'm sorry."

"Yeah, he started drinking and acting out. So, my grandfather decided that he needed a change of scenery. He fired him, and kicked us out."

Joely cringed. "That must have been terrible."

"For everyone involved." Holt wasn't sure why he was spilling this out. Maybe it was being back in the saddle again, riding the perimeter or maybe it was seeing Joe and Tony. Most likely it was because he liked talking with Joely and being back on the ranch made him feel raw and exposed, like a bad tooth. "But, my grandfather wouldn't have let his daughter and her children starve. He set Mel up as the manager of what's now the Palekaiko resort. I traded in my chaps for board shorts and the rest is history."

"You glossed over a few points."

He figured she'd see through that. "Yeah, well he was no better on the beach than he was in the fields. My mom left him when Mike was twelve and took him to Japan with her. I was seventeen and stayed with Mel. Someone had to look after him."

"Oh, Holt." She rubbed his leg.

He didn't want her sympathy, but his body zinged to attention at her touch. "When my grandfather died, Tetsuo took over and tried to take over the resort, but my grandfather left it to my mother—who would've been thrilled to see it burn to the ground. It got pretty bad. Well, you remember what it was like when you first got here."

"The locals loved us."

"Because we were cheap and on Kaanapali beach. Mel fucked off long before you showed up, though. Tetsuo was happy running it. Or at least having one of his gangsters run it." Holt stared out at Haleakala. The shield volcano was a comforting presence. No matter how things changed in his life, it was always there. When he was trying to fit in at Palekaiko, he could look up and see it. It had comforted him that he wasn't that far from home. It reminded him of happier days.

"The gangsters were the worst, though."

"Were they dangerous?" Joely asked, gripping the reins tighter.

"Not to me or Mike. Tetsuo would have drowned them out by Black Rock. But they hated Mel and would always try to make some extra money on the side."

"Like prostitution rings?"

Holt winced. "You are never going to forgive me for that, are you?"

"Why me? Out of all the maids, why did you think I was the one turning tricks?"

"Because you were the only one I thought would be worth paying for."

"I think that's a compliment," Joely said. "But I liked Tony's better."

"It wasn't meant as a compliment. I was trying to answer your question. You were secretive. You didn't let anyone get close to you. You were always getting excellent reviews from the tourists."

"I went the extra mile for them, but not the way you're thinking." She swatted him.

"I guess I underestimated the appeal of fresh towels."

"Damn straight."

"And I didn't think anyone else had the brains for it."

"I guess Selma was smarter than she looked." Joely stuck her tongue out at him.

"Not that smart. If she had given Tetsuo a cut, there would have been nothing I could do about it."

"Wait," she said. "Dude was in charge at that point. Well, as much as he oversaw anything before Amelia came."

"Didn't matter. Tetsuo still called the shots for a while. So, since Selma didn't fork over a percentage, he was happy to let the law step in."

Joely snorted. "Good riddance. I hated that bitch. She was a nasty piece of work."

"Why didn't you ever say anything? I was the head of security. You had to know I wasn't looking the other way."

"Because everyone knew and no one seemed to care."

"I cared."

"Besides, she threatened us."

"You definitely should have told me. You didn't have to live with that. I would have kicked that skanky bitch out just for that alone."

"She had friends." Joely shrugged. "It was easier to just let it be. Although, Kai and Makoa would take turns screwing around with the wheels on her cart, and Hani would take the batteries out of her walkie talkie so we didn't have to listen to her. Why didn't you figure it out?"

"I did. I was the one to catch her red handed."

"Of course, you thought you were catching me."

Holt smirked. "I was happy I didn't. Anyway, can you forgive me? I'm sorry I was suspicious of you."

She waved her hand at him. "I guess you had good reason. Why did your father sell the property to Dude and Marcus?"

"Something must have happened and Mel needed money fast without any questions."

"What do you mean?"

"I know he asked Tetsuo for a loan. Of course, Tetsuo turned him down. So as fuck you to Tetsuo, Mel sold the resort to Marcus and Dude. I found out about it the same time Tetsuo did." Holt shook his head. "Pissed doesn't even begin to describe it. Anyway, that was about seven years ago. I haven't seen Mel since."

"Where do you think he is?"

Holt shrugged. "Drunk somewhere. Maybe the Big Island working on a farm. How about you? Aren't your parents looking for you?"

"No. We're estranged." Her face scrunched up in anger. "I got married to Timothy to get away from them." She shook her head. "I was young and stupid."

"Did you try to contact them after Timothy put you in the hospital?" She was quiet for so long after that question, Holt had a feeling that the answer wasn't going to be a good one. "You don't have to talk about it, if you don't want to." He figured he should give her the same out she gave him.

Joely sighed. "No, but my sister, Sammy was able to help me."

"You have a sister?"

"Two of them," she said. "I had a brother, but he died."

"I'm sorry."

She blinked back tears. "It was a long time ago. Tanner was shot to death."

"That's awful. What happened?"

Taking off her ball cap, she ran her fingers through her hair. "Wrong place. Wrong time. He wasn't the target. My father was."

"Jesus," Holt said. "Did they catch the person who did it?"

"They?" Joely gave a half laugh. "No. *They* didn't. But Katie did."

"Katie?"

"My other sister. She's on death row at Santa Rita."

"Fuck." Holt was speechless. *I guess I don't have the market on really fucked up family dynamics.*

"Timothy didn't find out about any of this until after I married him. That was probably the beginning of the end for us. He was setting his sights on a career in politics. Having a jailbird for a sister-in-law puts a damper on things."

Holt nodded. He wondered if all this was what she had been keeping from all of them that made him think she was hiding something. She had been, but it was understandable.

70

"He tried to speed up her execution," she said in a small voice.

Holt's jaw dropped. He thought he disliked the senator before, now he'd like to take him on a boat ride and throw him to the sharks.

"But he couldn't do anything because it was out of his jurisdiction. But he tried. I hated him for that."

"You would think he would have welcomed the divorce."

"You'd think that. Unfortunately, he still thought he could control the narrative. Control me." Joely shook her head. "Can we take a rest?"

"Sure." He slid off his horse and helped her down. She was light as a feather when he put his hands on her waist and lifted her off Uma.

Joely held on to his shoulders as she steadied herself. "I'm not used to riding. It's hard to stand."

The horses kept walking.

"Uh, shouldn't we catch them?"

"They're going to go get something to drink at the pond." He pointed. "It's past that next hill. They'll be back when they want an apple."

"I thought the apples were for us," she said.

"Not unless you want to deal with a grumpy horse."

Chapter Nine

Holt took the backpack from her and unpacked, his head still reeling from their conversation. He watched as Joely spread out the blanket under a tree and opened the thermos, pouring them each a glass of POG juice. The pineapple, orange and guava was still ice cold. He drank two large glasses.

"The dust gets to you," he said, handing her a chicken curry salad sandwich.

He devoured his, having worked up an appetite and leaned back against the tree watching her stare out at the ocean far in the distance.

"Any word from Amelia?" she asked.

"Timothy still doesn't believe we're gone. He's conducting his own investigation."

"I don't like the sound of that."

"He's not going to get very far. No one knows where we are. Just that you're with me. And no one can connect me to this ranch without alerting Tetsuo. If it comes down to that, Timothy will have a lot more to worry about than his ex-wife."

She nodded. "Is he really as bad as they say he is?"

Today was the day for painful questions, but it was also one for honesty. "Yeah."

She nodded again. "It must have cost you a lot to ask him for us to stay here."

"Didn't cost me anything except for a few hours of hard work."

"That's not what I meant." Joely turned to him and pierced him with a look. "You want nothing to do with his illegal activities."

"The ranch is on the up and up. Trust me."

"I do," she said. "But by coming here, you're one step closer to working for him."

Sinking down onto his back, he folded his arms under his head. "I'm sure that's what he thinks. But this is not my home. The resort is."

Joely leaned over him. The ends of her ponytail tickled his cheek. "If something must be done about Timothy, I don't want you paying my debt."

"Nothing will be done about Timothy. No one is going to owe Tetsuo a debt. I won't allow it."

She poked him in the chest. "I can handle myself if it comes to it."

"Ow." He rubbed the spot. "You won't have to."

"Holt," she warned.

"Joely," he growled back.

She gave up and flopped next to him. "It's quiet up here. I keep expecting to see some tourists ride by and ask for more towels or something."

"Reason number two why Amelia shouldn't book tours up here." He hid a yawn behind his hand. He hadn't slept well last night. Too many memories. And dinner last night had been a strained affair because Tetsuo blew them off. He was glad. He hadn't felt up to sparring verbally with his uncle.

As his eyes drifted closed, he felt Joely prop herself up on her elbow and look at him.

"What?" he asked sleepily, wondering if there was something on his face.

"Thanks." Leaning over him, she kissed him on the mouth.

He probably shouldn't have parted her lips, but he did. She tasted like guava, which was his favorite. Turning on his side without breaking the kiss, he stroked his thumb across her cheek. Joely sidled in closer so their bodies were touching.

"You don't have to keep thanking me," he said. "But feel free to keep kissing me."

She scooted closer still. "All right," she whispered and pressed her mouth to his again.

Holt bit down on a groan, as he pulled her in. Her legs entwined with his and her arms wrapped around his neck. The little moans she was making in the back of her throat were driving him crazy. He could kiss her for hours. Rolling over on his back, he took her with him so she lay on top of him as their tongues dueled.

Running his hands down her back, he cupped her ass. Joely wiggled against his erection and the next thing he knew she was underneath him. He lifted his lips from hers to tease a trail of kissed along her jaw line. She tugged at the bottom of his shirt until he tossed it off. He was too impatient. As her hands travelled over his arms and back, he yanked up her T-shirt over her bra.

"You're so fucking gorgeous," he groaned before taking one of her nipples into his mouth.

Joely cried out, digging her nails into his shoulder. He lifted his head up to verify that it was pleasure in her eyes.

"Holt," she whispered. "Don't stop."

He wasn't planning on it. He sucked on one nipple while he tugged on the other. Grazing the sensitive peak with his teeth, Holt moaned when she lifted her hips and rubbed against him. Pushing back against her, they rocked together like teenagers. He licked down her belly, his fingers on the buttons of her jeans, when he heard hoofbeats.

It was probably Uma and Scout coming back from the pond.

But what if it wasn't?

"Damn it," he growled.

"What?" she asked.

Holt licked her belly button one last time, and she took in an excited breath. Pulling her shirt down, he kissed her warm mouth and rolled off her. "Someone's coming."

She gave a little scream and scrambled to a sitting position. Jamming her hat back on, she tried for a nonchalant pose as he searched for where he threw his shirt. He shrugged into it, but had to adjust himself.

He was half right. Uma came back. "Cock blocker," he muttered.

Joely laughed. "She just wants her apple." She stood up and reached into the backpack for it.

"Well, she's going to have to earn it." Holt hoisted himself into the saddle. "Let me go find the other juvenile delinquent and bring him back. Are you all right staying here by yourself?"

"Are you kidding me?" She laughed. "I'm going to take a nap. Or maybe read a book." She pulled out her phone. "It will be nice to relax. Thanks for making me feel so safe."

"I hope that's not all I make you feel," he said.

Her eyes twinkled at him. "We can talk about that later."

"We will." That was a damned promise.

Signaling Uma into a gallop, Holt admitted he was showing off just a bit. But the mare got into the spirit of things. Scout wasn't by the pond and Holt wondered if the horse just trotted back to the barn. That didn't make sense, though, because Uma would have gone with them.

As the terrain flattened out a bit, he caught a scent of wild lavender, and he turned his head to see where it was coming from. His gaze caught on movement in between a thick cluster of kauri pines and camphor trees that made up a small forest bordering their property with their nearest neighbors. He steered Uma towards it, wondering if they had poachers or a horse thief skulking around.

He didn't think to bring out a shotgun or a pistol because the four-legged predators were almost non-existent. Holt had forgotten about the two-legged kind. Still, there was a good chance there was nothing there and he was being overly suspicious. Loosely tying Uma up, he ducked through an opening in the forest.

Crouching down, he saw hoofprints. If they were Scout's, Holt couldn't figure out why the horse would have gone in on its own. He heard voices and saw that there was a makeshift clearing up ahead. As he approached, he recognized his brother's yurt. Trepidation swapped with annoyance.

"Damn it, Mike," he said, barreling into the makeshift camp. "You're lucky I didn't have my Glock. What the hell are you doing ... here?"

His brother stared at him with his arms crossed. "I could ask you the same question."

But Holt's attention was on the older man, who held Scout's reins and was brushing him. He wouldn't look at him and jammed his cowboy hat low on his face, but only an idiot wouldn't recognize their own father.

"I don't believe this shit." Holt snatched the reins out of Mel's hands and turned to lead the horse out of the clearing.

"What's your problem, Holt?" Mike said, pushing his chest into him.

"My problem is you rustled my horse." Holt effortlessly shoved him back.

"Your horse?" Mike trailed after him. "Since when do you come out here?"

"Since Joely and I are on vacation."

"Wait." Mike stopped dead in his tracks. "You and Joely? It's about time brah." He slapped him on the shoulder.

"What the hell does that mean?" Holt asked.

"Just what I said. She's been eyeing you for a long time."

"Don't be an ass." They were far enough away that when Holt lowered his voice he didn't think his father could over hear them. "What the fuck is he doing here?"

Mike's eyes rolled back in his head. "He got fired from his job on the Big Island. The foreman was a young punk who had it in for the older guys."

"I can't believe you're still buying his bullshit." Holt continued walking.

"It's not bullshit this time."

Holt made a frustrated noise in his throat trying to keep everything he wanted to say to his brother inside.

"He's been sober for two years."

Holt snorted.

"He's just here until he can get back on his feet again. Do you think Uncle Tetsuo would hire him?"

"Are you completely out of your fucking mind?" That one was so out of the realm of possibility, Holt had to stop in his tracks.

"Yeah." Mike jammed his hands into his board shorts. "I was thinking of seeing if there were any openings at the Palekaiko

Beach Resort. He'd get free room and board there as well as a job."

"You mean the resort that he used to own and ran into the ground, before selling it to the current owners?"

"You don't think that's a good idea? He has experience."

Shaking his head, Holt led Scout to the entrance. After untying Uma, he leapt into Scout's saddle. "Do what you want. Just leave me out of this. He's your responsibility. If Tetsuo catches you, I don't want to hear about it."

"You're not going to tell him?" Mike asked anxiously, running after the horses to keep up.

"There's not a chance in hell I'm going to open that can of worms."

"Awesome. Thanks brah, I knew I could count on you." Mike gave him the shaka.

Holt slowed the horse down and stopped. "Try not to get hurt. He can't be trusted. You know that."

"I believe him this time."

He tried. "Then you're almost as big of an idiot as he is."

Holt galloped away, trailing Uma after him.

His father was back, after all these years.

Just what he didn't need.

Chapter Ten

Joely was not cut out to be a cowboy, paniolo, whatever. Her ass was sore and her thighs weren't speaking to her. The sunburn on the back of her neck was deadly and she was covered with thick, red mud. She'd take cleaning toilets over this in a heartbeat.

When she literally fell asleep in the shower and almost drowned, she realized that trying to be macho was going to kill her.

After scrubbing her wet hair vigorously with a towel to dry it, she tossed on shorts and a tank top and went upstairs to Holt's room. He had been distant after he came back from rounding up Scout yesterday. Even though he said that something had come up that was bothering him, she couldn't help but wonder if he was regretting fooling around.

After all, instead of coming to her room last night, he excused himself early after dinner and went right to bed. Looking back, she probably should have done the same, instead of spending half the night on the internet trying to locate her sister. No luck on that front, but Timothy had taken the bait. Now, she just had to find a way to sneak out and catch a ride to Palekaiko on Thursday.

Joely knocked on Holt's door.

"Who is it?"

"It's me. Can I talk to you?"

She heard footsteps coming to the door and when Holt opened it up, she could see he didn't have anything on but a towel. "I-I can come back."

He looked behind her and down the hall. "Where's Kala?"

"She went out shopping."

"Have you seen Joe or Tony?"

"They said they were going back to the bunk house after lunch. That's what I wanted to talk to you…"

Holt yanked her into the room and closed the door.

"About," she whispered as he pressed her back against it.

"About?" he asked, leaning his arms on either side of her head.

Her throat went dry. "I forgot."

He bent his head and kissed her. Sweet heaven, he had a mouth on him. She slid her hands up his muscled torso and then around to his back, pulling him against her. Holt moaned low in his throat and grazed his hips against her belly. Tingles ran up and down her body as she rubbed up and down his erection.

"That's better. I meant to do that last night."

"Why didn't you?" she asked.

He closed his eyes and shook his head. "Some bullshit came up and I let it get to me. I'm sorry."

"That's okay. I was wondering if I had imagined where those kisses were going to take us." Joely's hands shook when she touched his well-defined biceps. She was having a hard time believing that this was finally happening.

"I think they're taking us right here."

"Good."

"I don't want you to think I'm taking advantage of you, though." Holt backed off slightly, but she wasn't having any of that nonsense.

"Oh, no you don't. I plan on taking full advantage. This is the first time in five years I don't have to look over my shoulder and wonder if someone is going to recognize me. It's the first time that you and I have been alone enough so we can explore …" She moved her hand back and forth between them. "… whatever the heck this is."

Smirking, Holt brushed his lips over her temple. "I know. I keep expecting Makoa to burst in on us looking for the banana boat or something."

Shaking her head, Joely giggled. "How can you misplace a twelve-foot inflatable banana?"

"He and Hani were probably monkeying around."

"Oh no," she said, ducking under his arm. "You did not start a pun war." Darting over to the bed, she grabbed a pillow and advanced on him. "That's not very appealing of you."

Holt lunged for her. Squealing, Joely jumped up on the bed.

"What are you? Yellow?" he asked.

"That was pretty lame." She threw the pillow at him, but he batted it aside. "Give it up. Your pun game is fruitless."

"You're lucky I like you a whole bunch."

"That's better," she said, grabbing the other pillow as she hopped off the bed. Holt circled around and she dove back on the bed, with the intention of rolling off the other side. But he was damned quick and grabbed her by the ankle and pulled her back.

"Look what I found in my bed. Speaking of peeling layers to get to the good parts, I think you're wearing too many clothes." Holt tugged on the waistline of her shorts and then paused like he was giving her a chance to call this off.

If she did, they could explain all of this away as just good friends blowing off steam. It was probably safer that way. She could very well have to leave in two weeks and Joely wanted to protect her heart.

"We don't have to do anything," he said.

He was so damned kind, she had to blink back tears. She didn't deserve him. But oh, how she wanted him. Would it be selfish to indulge in a crazy vacation love affair? She'd seen tourists hook up like that all the time. Then when it was time to go home, they went their separate ways.

"What if I want to do something?" she whispered.

Holt backed away from the bed. Joely was fascinated when he touched the towel that was wrapped around his waist.

"Last chance to change your mind," he said, and then dropped the towel.

Not bloody likely. She'd been fantasizing about this for years. Coming off the bed, she launched herself into his arms. The heck with protecting her heart. There was a handsome, naked man in front of her. She'd have to be an idiot to pass up this opportunity.

It would all sort out. One way or another. She would have no regrets.

Joely kissed him again, enjoying the feel of his muscled body pressed up against her. She laughed against his mouth when he picked her up and tossed her back on the bed.

Aches and pains? Never heard of them. He climbed on to the bed next to her. She flung off her top and bra while he helped her with her shorts and panties. And then they were skin to skin.

"I've been wanting to do this for a long time," he said.

"What stopped you?" she asked, breathlessly as he traced over her nipple with his fingertips.

Their lips brushed against each other and he moved on to kiss her chin, and then her neck. "I figured it would be awkward if you weren't interested."

He nipped gently at her neck, his big hands spread her legs wide. Leaning over her, she could feel his hard cock pressing into her hip. Unable to resist, she stroked her hand down his back to his fine, muscled ass.

When Holt captured her nipple in his mouth, she squeezed hard, almost digging her nails in. "I was interested," she squeaked out, ending on a moan as he tickled her nipple with his tongue as he sucked on it.

Holt stroked through the curls at the juncture of her thighs. He went on to the other nipple before sliding a finger in between her legs.

"Fuck," she whispered as he stroked his fingers through her hot, wetness. "I want you."

When he touched her clit, she gasped and her entire body jolted like she put her finger in an electrical socket. The soft tugging on her nipples and his slow rubbing of her clit made her whimper his name.

He let go her breast with one last suck and then plunged his tongue into her mouth. He flicked his finger faster and she held onto his shoulders while her hips rose to meet each pass. She slanted her mouth over his to deepen the kiss. Her hands roamed his body in a frenzy, but she couldn't get to his cock because it was pressed tightly against her body.

He fingered her into a slow orgasm, while his tongue played havoc with her senses. She slammed her thighs together as she came. Wave after wave of pleasure flooded through her and she shuddered, clutching his shoulders desperately.

"Been thinking about doing that the first day I saw you in your maid's uniform."

She chuckled breathlessly. "It's cotton polyester. I could see if it was a French maid's outfit, but it's really ugly."

"You wear it well. Still, I figured you'd get the wrong idea if I pinned you against the wall and stroked you to orgasm on your first day."

"I would have recovered," she said, running her fingers through his hair. "Can I touch you, now?"

"Please." Holt rolled onto his back and Joely stretched out on top of him.

Writhing against him, she enjoyed the hard planes of his muscles against her sensitive nipples. "You feel nice. I've been perving on your body ever since I saw you surf."

He lazily traced circles over her back, as she kissed him Pressing kisses against his jawline, she licked his earlobe before biting it. "I also had a lot of fantasies involving you, your handcuffs and me being bent over your desk."

Groaning, Holt would have rolled her over on her back, but she stopped him when she grabbed his thick cock.

"I can arrange that," he ground out.

She leaned up on her elbow and stroked him fast. She liked watching how his eyes flared and then regarded her under hooded eyelids. His nostrils flared and his breath quickened.

"It won't take much to get me to come in your hand," he said.

"How about my mouth?"

This time, she was flat on her back before she knew it.

"Not this time."

Reaching into his bedside drawer, he pulled out a condom.

"You bring a lot of girls back here?" she asked.

"You're the first." He ripped the package open with his teeth and rolled it on his cock.

"Why the supply in the drawer then?"

"Boy Scout, remember?" Then he pushed inside her and Joely forgot everything except the sweet rocking of his body against hers.

Entangling her legs with his, she kissed him as the pleasure built up inside her again. His cock fit her snugly. Each thrust zinged sensations through her that had her wild and trembling.

"Joely, Joely," he moaned, sounding as out of his mind as she was.

She hadn't expected their first time to be so sensual and loving. She was used to quick fucks against the walls and back seat blow jobs. Being flat on her back in the world's most comfortable bed was luxury. The scent of lavender from the flower arrangement on his bureau and the view of Haleakala out his window, just added to the luxury.

"Holt," she cried out as she came around his cock.

To her surprise, he pulled out. But before she could say anything, he flipped her on her stomach.

"Get on all fours," he said in a voice rich with passion.

On shaking hands, she did what he asked and this time when he thrust into her, she cried out at the intensity. Gone was the sweet, slow love making. Holt fucked her with a single-minded persuasion that had her clutching the sheets.

Joely let out a low moan, her tortured nerve endings on fire from two orgasms. Now, her body was going into overdrive, not knowing what to expect.

"Yes," she cried out. "Fuck me. Just like that."

Holt made a sound that was part growl and part grunt and her insides liquefied. Joely held on for dear life as he took her hard and fast, each thrust pushing her closer to madness. Throwing her hair over her shoulder, she looked at him. His eyes were intense and the smile on his face was deliciously evil.

"Do you like this?"

"Yes." She nodded.

"Is this how you wanted to be fucked over my desk?"

"Yes!"

He gave a dry chuckle that she felt in the tightening of her nipples.

"We'll have to play around in my office sometime."

Images from her imagination assaulted her senses and she clamped down on his cock. He cried out, his fingers digging into her ass and with a few more hard pumps, he groaned and shook. Releasing into her, Holt's body slowed as he still pushed in and out.

"Finally," he said, dropping a kiss between her shoulder blades. "I should have done this a year ago."

"At least," she agreed, rolling over on her back as he got up to dispose of the condom.

He cuddled her against him when he came back. "Have I mentioned I love your breasts?" He thumbed her nipple, while giving one a squeeze.

She leaned up to lick at his earlobe again. "You're lucky I'm too sore from being on horseback. Otherwise I'd ride *you* into the sunset."

He pulled her on top of him anyway. Joely rested her head on his chest and enjoyed his big hands soothing over her.

"How was your first day as a paniolo?" he asked.

"It sucks. I can't handle it. I'm going to cry," she said in a sleepy voice.

"Really?" he said, stroking her cheek with his finger.

Suppressing a shiver, she put her arms around him. "No, not really. But I'm no good out there."

"You'll get better."

"I'd rather stay behind and cook and clean. It's what I do." She shrugged. "Tell me the guys wouldn't want a maid to do their laundry and clean the barracks."

Holt barked out a laugh. "Honey, those guys are pigs."

"It's nothing I'm not used to. And besides, I'm slowing them down."

She knew she had him by the chagrined look that briefly passed over his face. She saw the rolled eyes and the sneers. The paniolos didn't dare say anything outright to her because Holt had made it obvious that she was his guest. But the contempt didn't sit well with her.

"Look, I know I could learn how to do this given the time and training, but we're only going to be here two weeks. I want to be where I can help out the most, not make more work."

"It's not really much of a vacation for you if you're busy picking up after ten guys."

87

"I'm all right with it. I'll finish long before you guys get back for lunch, and I can help Kala with the cooking. I can still get some R&R in."

"If you're sure?"

She nodded. "Definitely."

"Then I think I can arrange it."

"Just don't work too hard during the day," Joely said, dropping a kiss on his cheek. "I've got evening plans for you."

Holt grinned. "Don't worry about me." He rolled her underneath him again.

Chapter Eleven

Joely went back for another shower before dinner. All she wanted to do was go to bed. While she didn't have to be up at four a.m. tomorrow, it had been a busy day.

An exhausting day. Her eyes fluttered shut and a goofy smile stretched across her face. Wait until she told Amelia and Michaela. Amelia would give her a high five and do a happy dance. Michaela would say, "It's about time."

"It was about time," Joely murmured.

As she changed into a sundress for dinner, her phone buzzed. It was an answer to her craigslist ad. Sitting down on the edge of the bed, she read the message.

Sounds perfect. I'd like to arrange a time to see the place.

She didn't recognize the number or the name. It could be anyone, but her gut said it was from her family. There wasn't any code attached to it to make sure. Whoever was writing this wanted to meet with her.

Joely didn't want to risk that it was her parents, but she didn't have a choice. She wrote back:

Alexandria is off the market, but if you're interested in a similar place. I can show you one on Maui. The town of Makawao. I'll be showing the place on Friday around noon. Shall we meet by the post office?

If it was a person who really wanted an apartment in Alexandria, they would either not respond or say no. It was only Tuesday, so if this message was from her family, they would be able to make arrangements to get to Maui by Friday. She would go to the block party with Holt and if her parents showed up by the post office, she'd leave before they saw her. But if it was Sammy…

Joely stifled a sob. She hadn't seen her sisters in years. It would be good to see Sammy again. That reminded her that she should put money into Katie's commissary account. She usually did it on the first of the month, but if things started heating up, she didn't want her sister to go without.

Of course it was possible, if not probable, that Timothy had managed to crack her parents' code. Which was even more reason why she had to get to Palekaiko on Thursday night. That way she could be prepared for whatever happened on Friday.

She felt a little guilty about dragging another one of her friends into this mess, but if there was one person she could count on to help her out, it was Makoa.

"*Aloha wahine*," he said. "How goes hiding out from the bad guy?"

"It's an experience. I was wondering if you've got some time off coming? I was hoping to catch some waves on Thursday."

"Why don't I come up to you? We can do Hookipa."

Ugh, no. Holt would tag along if they did that. As it was, she was going to feel guilty about ditching him. She'd have to time it that Makoa picked her up before he got back from herding cattle, but after she finished her own chores.

"I was missing the waves down by Lahaina. Any chance you can pick me up and bring me back down? I can find my own way back Upcountry afterwards."

"Why can't Holt take you down?"

It was a good question. Holt wouldn't let her break and enter into Timothy's room, and he sure as hell wouldn't let her hack into her ex's computer. "Ah, he's got to work."

"That's a bummer. But I don't have a ride."

"Can you borrow one?" she asked, hope fading away.

"Nah, usually I could grab one of the resort's vans but they're all booked for the rest of the week."

Well, shit.

"All right, maybe some other time this week." Joely sighed.

"Roger dat."

She was reluctant to get off the phone with him. It shocked her how much she missed the resort, and she'd only been away for a few days. "How are things over there?"

"Busy. Dude's slackin' off. Amelia's got us runnin' ragged. The usual."

"How are the waves?" she asked, nostalgic.

"The storm surge has been pretty rough. No sharks though."

"That's good." That was the one thing Joely didn't miss about surfing. She tried not to think about the other animals she was sharing the ocean with—especially not the ones with big teeth.

"How are the guests doing? Did Mrs. D'Angelo in 301 get her fresh flowers delivered."

"Every day. My cousin is thrilled for the business. Thanks for recommending her."

"Anytime," Joely said. "And the luaus? Are they running smooth?" Ever since Holt's brother Mike left, they hadn't been as well organized.

"Yeah, Amelia got some of the kids involved. A few seniors are interning for her and helping out."

"Wow, that's a great idea." Joely hoped Timothy would just go home already. She wanted her home and her friends. The ranch and Holt were a fantastic substitute, but she longed to stop running and put down roots. She had started to at Palekaiko.

"That asshole, though. The one you're running from? He's been asking about you. No one here has said anything. Not even Cami. But you better come back quick, because she's bucking for your job."

She can have it.

Joely missed the beach, but she didn't miss being the head of housekeeping. She liked cleaning rooms, and then having her entire day free. Having to deal with staffing issues had been a real bummer.

"Do you think he's going to leave next week?" she asked.

"The old guy? Yeah, I know we ain't gonna give him another room. But will he go home? Who knows?"

Joely could almost picture him shrugging. "Well, let's hope for the best." And plan for the worst.

"Always do. Take care of yourself and go easy on Holt."

"What do you mean?" Joely cocked her head to the side.

"I mean, he's been in love with you for years. Don't break his heart."

Love?

She barely registered getting off the phone with Makoa. Love was a whole other ball park. She wasn't in the right place to have a relationship like that. The thought of hurting Holt was almost a physical pain. But this was Makoa, who told her. Sweet, lovable, and not too bright, Makoa. Maybe he saw the mutual attraction between her and Holt, and just took it to mean it was love. Makoa was a romantic that way.

92

Rubbing the sudden pain in her chest, she slipped on a pair of sandals. She didn't deserve to be loved. Not when she was hiding shit from the people who cared for her. She should probably move on regardless of whether Timothy did or not. It was the safe thing to do.

As she walked down to dinner, she wondered why she felt so giddy. Could Holt really love her? Could she love him?

Joely forced that thought down where it couldn't bubble up again and take her by surprise. She had no reason thinking about a permanent relationship when her sister might be on the way with a new passport and a new identity for her.

"I hate this thing." Kala pounded her fingers into her laptop. "The connection is so slow."

"Maybe you should go back to Wailea," Holt said innocently. "Your condo gets great reception."

They were standing in the family room. Holt was mixing martinis while Kala sat at her desk and scowled at the computer.

Kala ignored him. "It's not just that. It keeps locking and I get the green screen of shame."

"Huh?"

"I think she means the blue screen of death," Joely said, walking in. Peering over Kala's shoulder, she saw some strange flashes in the corner of the screen. "What's that?" Joely pointed.

"I don't know. It always does that."

"That's not right. Can I take a look?"

Kala shrugged. "Sure."

"When was the last time you ran a virus protection on this?"

"We've got a subscription that takes care of that."

Joely grunted and checked it out. While it was up-to-date, she knew that it didn't always catch the newest worms or other computer viruses. She downloaded a more aggressive program and then went to work.

"Holy key logger, Batman," she said.

"What's going on?" Holt handed her a martini. It was mango and rum. It went down nice. She would have liked to be sharing a pitcher of these all alone with him, but Kala had come back a few hours ago with enough food to feed an army for a month. Joely didn't think she was going anywhere.

"Is there a problem?" Kala said in her ear.

So much for a little alone time.

"Yeah, this laptop is crawling with data miners and information collectors. Everything you do is being recorded."

"Can you stop that?"

They all turned at the deep, masculine voice from the back of the room. Joely swallowed hard. It wasn't the first time that she met Tetsuo Hojo, but there had been a lot of other people around and his attention hadn't been directed at her.

"Yeah," she said. "Piece of cake."

As she scrubbed the offending software, she was aware that Holt hitched a hip on the desk and was sticking close. Kala and Tetsuo were having a quiet argument in the corner.

"There, that should do it," she said, starting to stand up.

"Can you track the origin of the spyware?" Tetsuo asked.

Joely thought about it. "Not all of it. But maybe..."

She dug a little deeper into the code of a few of the quarantined bugs. "Looks like the usual Russian worms. This one is from

Africa. This key logger comes from a social media quiz, like which flower are you?"

Kala, apparently, was a rose.

"But where is it going to?" Tetsuo asked.

"A database somewhere."

"What are they looking for?" Kala piped up.

"Information to sell," she said shortly. "People will pay good money for email addresses and their shopping lists."

"How much money?" Tetsuo said.

"Uncle," Holt warned.

"Depends on who's buying and how many names."

"Is someone selling my information?"

"Not anymore." Joely rebooted the computer. "It should run a lot faster now and you shouldn't see any more of that flickering code across the screen. If you do, just run the Flyswatter app I installed."

"How do I do that?" Kala asked.

"I'll show you once it boots up." When the screen flashed to the startup screen, Joely caught a little blip. "Son of a bitch."

"What?" Tetsuo said, coming closer.

"One of the bugs came back. It shouldn't have been able to get out of quarantine. Unless…"

"Unless what?" Tetsuo said, and the quiet menace in his voice made the hairs stand up on her arms.

"Uncle," Holt warned again.

"Can I take your laptop apart? I promise to put it back together."

"Have you done this before?" Kala asked. "This is a very expensive laptop."

Joely snorted. "It's a piece of shit." Then winced. "Sorry. While this may have been expensive, it's a very basic model. Yeah, I've done this thousands of times. I built my own computer from parts once."

"I didn't know that," Holt said.

"Why are you working as a maid, then?" Tetsuo regarded her thoughtfully.

"Uh." He had her there. "Let me just run upstairs and get my tools."

She took the stairs two steps at a time. This was stupid. She shouldn't have shown them she was computer savvy. Still, Joely couldn't deny that her insides were fluttering with excitement and she felt alive. It was like making love with Holt, only less orgasmic and easier on her sore muscles.

Grabbing her kit, she flew back down the stairs. After a few twists with her micro screw driver, she was removing the hard drive. "There you are, you bastard," she said, using a tweezers to take out a mini recording device.

"Let me see that." Tetsuo held out his hand and she dropped it in his palm.

After giving the rest of the parts a thorough look over, Joely put it all back together again and rebooted the machine. "That's better," she said.

"How did this get on my machine?" Tetsuo asked.

Joely got up from showing Kala how to activate the malware detector app and gestured for Holt to pour her another martini.

"I don't know. Kala, how long have you been having problems with the computer?"

"Months now."

"Did you take it in for servicing?"

"No, but I had that nice man who takes care of our gardens take a look at it."

Tetsuo cursed. "I need his name."

"I'll get his card." Kala bustled out of the room.

"I appreciate your help on this," Tetsuo said. "I may need you to look at a few of my other computers."

"No Uncle," Holt said.

"It's all right." Joely put a hand on Holt's arm. "Sure, I'd be glad to. It's the least I can do now that I won't be riding after cattle before dawn."

"You're cleaning the barracks, that's more than enough."

"Yeah, but this stuff is fun for me."

Tetsuo nodded. "If you'll excuse us." He hurried after his wife.

"I don't want you getting involved in his business," Holt said.

"I can't really say no. He's allowing me to stay here rent free."

"You and I are working to earn our keep. After dinner, you and Kala are going to put together a crockpot oatmeal breakfast along with some breakfast sandwiches that we can reheat."

"That seems like cheating."

"You want to get up at three a.m. to cook?"

"You know," Joely said. "The microwave works just fine for me."

Holt walked over to the study door and looked out. He closed it behind him.

"Oh no you don't," she warned him. "I won't be able to walk tomorrow."

"Blame it on the horse." He took her in his arms and kissed her.

She tried to stay firm, but it felt too damn good. It was like they were making up for lost time. Joely couldn't help but think that if these were the last two weeks together, she should work on making memories.

Her phone buzzed, cutting things off before things got too heated.

"I should see who's calling?" she said breathlessly. She was a hair away from begging him to take her on the desk.

Looking down at the text, Joely felt her smile freeze in place on her face.

See you noon on Friday, Sis.

Chapter Twelve

Things were finally falling into place. According to Holt's sources at Palekaiko, Timothy was digging up a whole lot of nothing about him and Joely. Mike and Mel had taken off. Holt wasn't sure when, but when he went back to check, his brother's yurt was gone. Tetsuo and Kala went back to Wailea to confront the gardener about what he did or did not do to Kala's laptop. This left Holt and Joely completely alone in the house, which is what he had planned for all along.

"You gonna sit there grinning like an idiot or are you going to go after that calf?" Joe snarled at him.

Knowing better than to argue, Holt rode off after the stray and herded him back up front where its mother was. It was like he never left. Sure, his thighs were screaming from being in the saddle for hours, but being on top of a horse was as natural to him as breathing.

"Give him some slack. He and his girl are probably up all night playing checkers or something."

"Watch it, Tony," Holt warned.

"I'm just saying, if I had a pretty wahine like that cleaning my house and making me breakfast, I'd marry the girl. Am I right, fellas?"

Holt rolled his eyes. Whatever ill feelings they had toward Joely's inexperience on a horse, faded away when they saw what she did to the bunk house.

While he busted his ass with fencing and taking care of the cattle, Joely put a spit shine on the barracks. At first they grumbled about having their space invaded, but even the crustiest of cowboys commented that it was nice to have a woman's touch.

"There are hospital corners on my bed."

"And fresh sheets."

"It smells like pine in here."

The paniolos were offended, embarrassed, and pleased as all get out. All the little touches Joely had done brightened up their living quarters. It's what made her such a good employee at the Palekaiko resort. She knew how to make people happy.

Holt was getting back into the swing of things on the ranch. The early mornings never bothered him like they did his brother. There were even times this week when Holt forgot he had another life and a job waiting for him at the beach resort.

"She's probably looking for a husband who doesn't live in a box by the ocean." Joe was about as subtle as an enraged bull seeing a red cape. He was looking to retire, and Holt knew that he didn't want any of the paniolos who worked with him to take over.

Holt had a pretty good idea who he wanted to pass the reins over to, but that wasn't going to happen. That horse had escaped the pen a long time ago. Actually, it had been pulled out kicking and screaming. But in the end, the result was the same.

"Speaking of cooking, what's for lunch?"

Kala had left a fully stocked fridge and freezer. "Joely's making a huge pot of chili and loaves of cornbread for lunch. Dinner's a cookout on the grill with different side dish salads."

The guys approved and once they finished for the morning and headed back to the ranch house, the devoured Joely's lunch like they hadn't eaten in weeks. Holt was surprised when Joe pulled her aside afterwards. Curiosity got the best of him, and Holt wandered over to shamelessly eavesdrop on their conversation.

"If you slice them up and toss them on the grill with some peppers and onions, I can take care of the rest."

"Fantastic. And I'll make a few trays of lasagna. All you'll have to do is warm them up."

Joe put his arm around Joely. "Better make it a few dozen trays."

"What are you two up to?" Holt asked.

Joely looked away as if he caught her doing something wrong.

"Nothing," Joe said. "Just you two have earned the day off tomorrow. Joely's going to cook up *choke* steaks tonight so we can have steak and cheese for lunch tomorrow, and her world famous lasagna for dinner."

"I wouldn't say that, but it is pretty tasty."

"Take the compliment when you can, sistah," Joe said and kissed her on the top of the head.

"Don't screw this up." Joe hit him in the chest when he passed by. "I like her."

Holt shook his head. "He's something else."

"I think he's sweet," Joely said.

"Then, sistah, you haven't been payin' attention." Holt mimicked Joe's voice and caught the dish towel she whacked him with.

Because the guys were heading back out to their horses, he risked a kiss. After she leaned against him, Holt realized he was covered in dirt.

"Sorry," he said, breaking away.

"I don't mind getting dirty." She winked at him and sashayed back into the kitchen.

Oh, so that was how it was. He moved to follow her, but was caught up short by Tony clearing his throat.

"We got work to do."

Holt stifled his groan. Tony was almost as bad as Uma at cockblocking. "Roger dat," he said, with one longing look at Joely's backside.

"She'll be here waiting for you when you get back."

Holt was taken aback at how right that felt. He allowed himself a small fantasy. What would it be like to be the foreman on his uncle's ranch?

Would Joely consider leaving the beach for this?

Would he?

***

After the cowboys ate their weight in beef, they staggered back to the bunk house. Holt helped Joely clean up in the kitchen.

"The lasagna smells good." He peeked inside the oven and even though he didn't think he could eat another bite, the bubbling cheese had him reconsidering.

"Do you think five trays will be enough?" She fretted, tugging at her apron.

"That's a half a tray per person. Plus, garlic bread. I think by the time these two weeks are over, they'll be too fat to ride."

"I like cooking," she marveled. "I've forgotten that."

"Yeah," Holt said, pouring them both a glass of wine. "When you've got a buffet breakfast and lunch and luau leftovers every night, there's no need to cook."

Stretching and wincing, Joely rubbed the back of her neck. "I'm beat."

"Let's go into the living room and watch a movie."

"I'm going to fall asleep." She smiled, but took her glass and followed him.

Holt tossed a pillow on the floor. "Here, sit on that and I'll give you a massage."

"Don't have to ask me twice." She settled in between his legs and leaned back against the couch.

Tagging a big swig of his wine, he put it aside. "This would be better if you take off your shirt."

"Better for whom?"

"Both of us."

She craned her neck to look back at him. "Go lock the door. I don't want Joe or Tony coming in for a midnight snack."

"You got it."

Holt couldn't believe his luck. Finally, they were going to spend a nice quiet evening all alone. Locking the door, he popped back into the kitchen for the bottle of wine.

However, when he got back into the living room Joely was snoring like a kitten with her face mushed up against the couch.

Oh well, this was nice too. He poured the wine back into the bottle and jammed the cork back in. There was always tomorrow. Gently, so as not to wake her, Holt lifted her up in his arms and carried her to her bedroom.

After tucking her in, he went downstairs to make reservations to see the sunrise at Haleakala. Looking at his watch, Holt figured if they got up at two a.m., they should be there in time. It was just a little past eight now, so that would give them a good six hours of sleep.

After taking a quick shower, Holt crawled into bed with her. He stifled a yawn with the back of his hand. Joely mumbled something in her sleep and turned so she was in his arms. As he drifted off, he stroked her silky hair wishing she was naked against him. But then again, they wouldn't be sleeping if she was.

He could definitely get used to this.

Holt allowed himself the fantasy again. He wasn't a security guard at a tourist resort, where the most exciting thing that happened was separating a few drunks.

He was a foreman in charge of four thousand acres of land and ten ornery paniolos. Smiling, he pictured seeing Joely in the kitchen in the morning. Maybe, he'd take a long lunch and make love to his wife in the afternoon.

Wife?

Holt's eyes flashed open and he stared at the ceiling. Where the hell had that come from? Joely muttered something that sounded like meatballs and turned over. He spooned into her as he thought about Joe's words.

What did a security guard have to offer a wife? He tried to picture them living at the Palekaiko resort. If he had been a billionaire like Dude or Marcus, they could live on his yacht or in the owner's suite. Since he wasn't, they'd share a room about the size of the ranch's guest bedroom.

Or they could give up the free room and board and get a place on their own. But that was expensive. Still, he had some money saved up.

Shaking his head, Holt closed his eyes. He was jumping the gun. It was still too early in their relationship, if even that's what they had, to start thinking about marriage.

Still…

Holt held Joely close. He could get used to this.

***

Jesus, who was the asshole who set the alarm for two in the morning?

Oh.

Holt groaned.

That would be him.

"No," Joely moaned. "It's our day off."

He was tempted to fall back into bed, but the thought of sharing the sunrise at ten thousand feet with Joely was an opportunity he didn't want to miss.

"Come on sleepy head. We're going to Haleakala."

"Is it erupting?" Joely's voice was muffled from the pillow she had over her head.

"No, I want to show you the sunrise."

"I've seen it," she said sourly.

"Not from up there you haven't. Come on, take a quick shower and get going. We want to get a parking space."

"We do?" She yawned.

"Come on, sleepyhead. We'll have all day to sleep."

"Promise?" she grumbled.

"I promise." When she didn't move, he said, "Don't make me carry you into the shower."

"All right. All right. I'm going."

She probably thought he didn't see the tongue she stuck out at him. He hurried upstairs to change into jeans and a T-shirt.

Joely surprised him because she was downstairs waiting for him. "It's cold."

He tossed her one of his hoodies. "Put this on. I've also got a blanket in the car."

Opening the car door for her, he draped the wool blanket over her lap. "I feel like such a lightweight," she said. "I'm usually coming home from the club at this hour."

He got behind the wheel. "When was that?"

She yawned so wide, he was afraid she was going to crack her jaw. "In my head, it was just a few weeks ago. But now that you mention it, the last time I was awake at this hour was Marcus and Michaela's wedding."

"I remember. You danced with me."

"I was trying to seduce you, but I drank too much."

"If you were sober, I would have been happily seduced."

"If I was sober, I wouldn't have had the nerve to ask you to dance." She leaned her head on his shoulder. "Why didn't you ask me to dance before I let Makoa talk me into trying his Auntie's home brew."

"You drank that?"

"It only hurts your stomach on the first glass. After that you don't feel a thing."

"Literally."

She nodded. "Don't change the subject." She poked him in the leg.

"I thought you were with Makoa."

"What?" Joely jolted upright. "Why?"

"You're always together."

"He's my friend. We're usually with Kai and Hani too."

Holt turned on the heater and pulled out on the highway. It was near deserted this time of night, and it was hard to concentrate on the road. "I should have brought some coffee."

"Amateur," she said, and reached in the back for a Thermos. After pouring him a cup, she smirked.

"Beauty and brains," he said, inhaling the aroma. "I don't know how I missed smelling the coffee brewing."

"It's pretty early in the morning, even for a hunky paniolo like you."

"Thanks for coming with me. I really wanted to share this with you."

She snuggled back up to him. "Too bad the sunrise has to start so early in the morning."

"Don't you want a cup?" he asked.

"I'm going to take a nap. Wake me when we're on top of the world."

"Will do."

Joely snoozed all the way up to the peak.

He couldn't blame her, but he knew it would be worth it once she saw it. She'd love all the colors. It was breathtaking. He remembered when his Mom and Dad took him and Mike up here.

That was before everything turned to shit. It was a magical morning, just the four of them.

When they got to the park, Holt paid the entrance fee on his credit card. He had managed to get his wallet out of his pants without waking Joely. They still had a half hour of driving to go and it was straight up another three thousand feet. He was glad he had the coffee because the road became very windy and he needed all his wits about him.

Checking the temperature on the dash, Holt turned on the heat. Forty-six was a cold morning.

"Wake up, Sleeping Beauty."

"I'm awake."

"Then why are your eyes closed?"

Joely wrapped the blanket around her and got out of the car without answering him. He went around to the trunk to pull out the two beach chairs he had brought.

"Grab the coffee," he said.

As they walked from the parking lot to the viewing area, Holt was glad they had beat the tourist buses up and had their pick of spots. He set up the chairs facing east.

"I'm freezing," she said, her teeth chattering.

"Come here and sit on my lap."

She gave him a suspicious look, but came over. Unpeeling some of the layers, he held her close to him. Joely yawned loudly in his ear.

"It's still dark."

He kissed her chilled cheek. "You can snooze a little bit more. I'll wake you up when it starts to get light out."

She jumped when he slid his hand up her shirt.

"Your hands are cold."

"Sorry. Let me warm them up." He unbuttoned her jeans and pulled the zipper down.

"Holt," she whispered, scandalized.

"There's no one here. Yet." Dipping his hand inside her underwear, he rubbed his finger between her legs.

Squirming, she bit his earlobe.

"Oh, you want to play?" He turned his head and kissed her, thrusting his tongue inside her eager mouth. Wet heat flooded over his finger and he flicked another finger inside her.

Joely moaned in his mouth.

Holt heard the bus chug up the mountain and he rubbed faster, wanting her to come before they were caught.

She held on to his shoulders, her mouth never leaving his. He could hear her slick wetness as he circled around her clit, fast and hard. Joely jerked in his arms and pushed her legs together.

"Oh Holt," she whispered, a soft tremor going through her.

He touched her gently then, as she cried out against his mouth. When the first door slammed, Joely straightened up and fumbled with her pants.

She leaped off him and settled into her own chair.

"Warmed up?" he asked, licking his finger. She tasted like musk and peaches and he couldn't wait for some privacy to explore her further.

"I'll say. Too bad we were interrupted."

Holt shifted in his chair. "We've got all day." If he hadn't been watching her, he wouldn't have noticed the slight frown across her face. Or the way her teeth worried at her lower lip. "Are you all right?"

She took in a deep breath. "Yeah. I'm fine. Just tired. I guess. Do you think we could risk going back down to Lahaina?"

"Why? You want to surf?"

"Yeah," she said, brightly.

It didn't feel right. She was so terrified of Timothy, why would she want to go back after only six days? "We can go to Hookipa."

"The locals hate me." Joely grimaced.

"Nah, they forgot all about you and that bonehead move you pulled on the reef."

"I miscalculated the wave," she said hotly. "I'm human."

"You almost tore your arm off."

"Felt like I did." She rubbed it. "Still got the scars. Fucking coral. Ruined a good day of surfing too. I was out of the water for almost a month."

"Well, that's not going to happen again. Besides, you'll be with me. I'll keep you safe."

"I know you would." She reached over to hold his hand. "I know." Joely let out a big sigh.

Holt couldn't wait until all this was over and they could get back to their lives. He didn't like feeling so conflicted over where he belonged. He wanted to go back to being a security chief and Joely being the head of housekeeping. Then they could start this relationship off right, without any secrets or hidden dangers. He squeezed her hand reassuringly. Just a little more than a week. They could do that.

The sunrise was at five-fifty a.m. It was like someone turned on the lights, but instead of the normal blue sky it was as if all the colors in the world spilled out of a paint box.

Joely caught her breath. "We're higher than the clouds. It's almost like we're on another planet. Are you sure we didn't fly to Mars while I was asleep?"

Holt wrapped his arms around her and rested his chin on the top of her head. "Worth losing a few extra Zs for?"

"Definitely. I feel like my problems are so small up here far away from everything."

He hugged her. "You don't have to worry about Timothy. I'm not going to let anything happen to you."

She stiffened in his arms and he wondered what he said that was so wrong.

"Can we go back to Palekaiko?" she said in a small voice.

His heart sank. "You don't like the ranch?"

"What? No, that's not it." She turned around in his arms. "I forgot a few things and I wanted to go back to my room and grab them. We'll be in and out. Timothy won't even know we're there."

Holt frowned. "You want to go now?"

"No," she said. "I'm too tired. I'm afraid my reflexes would be off. I figured we could go tonight around dinner time. We can circumvent the luau. You can keep watch while I get my things."

"It's risky," he said. It also didn't make sense. Six days ago, she hotwired a bike to get away from this guy. "What if he sees you?"

"He won't."

Holt was glad that she was feeling more confident, but he didn't want to risk their plan. It was imperative that Timothy thought she was off the island. "No, tell me what you want and I'll go and get

111

it. If he sees me, I'll tell him you left me and went to California or something."

Joely bit her lip and looked away.

"I know you're frustrated," he said. "But we'll get through this. We just have to play it safe. It's just for a few more days."

She nodded. "You're right."

"I'm always right." Holt smiled and turned her around so she faced the sunrise. He hugged her tight. "We're going to get through this."

Joely sighed. "I know."

She didn't sound as happy as he thought she would about that.

Chapter Thirteen

What the hell was she going to do? Joely didn't have a chance of ditching Holt when he was in watch dog mode. Part of her was really thrilled about that, and the other part of her wanted to roll down the window of his Accord and scream. She worked so hard to be able to leave the ranch today.

It was Thursday, and Timothy was going out to dinner at Lahaina's hot new restaurant on her dime. It would be all worth it—if she could get to his computer. But there was no way she could get there, short of stealing Holt's car.

She was a little ashamed that she was actually considering it. Somehow, she thought that Holt wouldn't be appeased by a macadamia nut pie the way Dude had been.

"You're quiet," he said as they pulled back into the ranch.

As much as it put a crimp in her plans, she loved seeing the sunrise over Haleakala and then hiking for a bit. They had stopped for lunch on the way down, and any other day, she would be looking forward to spending the rest of the day lounging in bed with Holt. But now, she'd have to hope he fell asleep and was a sound sleeper, so he didn't wake up until after she stole his car.

Which would really put a damper on their second date. Oh well, there was always the block party on Main Street tomorrow. If she could pull off getting to the Palekaiko Beach Resort and back by the time he woke up.

"Just tired, I guess." Tired of lying. Tired of doing illegal things just to survive. Tired of running. Finally, when it seemed like her friendship with Holt was growing into something deeper, there was still the shadow of her ex-husband over them.

There were days when she thought her sister Katie had the right of it. If Timothy drowned snorkeling by Molokini, Joely's problems would be over.

Was she that far gone into the dark side, that she was wishing for Timothy's death? The thought shamed her, yet she couldn't deny that all she would feel was relief.

"This is not fucking happening," Holt growled.

For a moment, Joely thought he knew. That somehow, he figured out that she was planning on getting back to the resort by any means tonight.

Joely opened her mouth to explain, but realized he wasn't looking at her. She followed his gaze to the side of the driveway. His brother Mike was standing there with an older man. They were mounted on horses.

Mike gave them the shaka. He looked like a skinnier version of Holt—if Holt covered himself with surfer tats, dyed his hair red, and styled it in a mohawk. Mike looked like a drowsy parrot. The older man next to him could have been one of the ranch hands, but she didn't recognize him. He hadn't been eating at the table in the main house with the rest of the paniolos.

He sat on the horse like he spent most of his life there and his boots and jeans were coated with the red Maui dirt. His expression flickered from anger to sadness and then resignation.

"Don't you fucking dare," Holt called out of the window and shut off the car.

Mike slid off his horse and gestured for the older man to do the same.

"Stealing horses? Are you out of your mind? How far did you think you were going to get?" Holt was enraged. Joely had never seen him lose his cool before. It was a little scary.

114

She stumbled out of the car, which drew all their attention. Shit. That was the last thing she wanted was to be on the receiving end of Holt's temper.

"Howzit, Joely," Mike said.

"Hey." She nodded back.

"This is my Dad." Mike gestured with his thumb.

Oh.

Oooooh.

"Hi," she managed to get out on the third try.

"You need to leave," Holt said, taking his father by the arm.

"That's what we were doing," his father said, shaking him off.

The two men glared at each other and Joely could see the family resemblance in their set jaws and angry stances.

"You can't steal Tetsuo's property. He'll kill you."

Somehow, Joely didn't think Holt was exaggerating.

"We were going to borrow them," Mike said when his father just continued to glare at Holt.

"Ri-ight," Holt drew out the word. "Where were you going?"

"As far as we could," Mike answered. "Into town where he could get a cab to Palekaiko."

Joely perked up at that. This could be a blessing in disguise. Holt would be too distracted by his father to wonder what she was up to. "Maybe, we should drive your father there," she said.

"Good idea," Holt said. "You and Mike take the horses back to the barn. I'll be back once I drop my father off. What do you want me to get from your room while I'm there?"

Shit. Shit. Shit.

"Text me when you get there and I'll tell you what to look for," she said, stomping over to where Mike had the horses.

Holt half dragged his father to the car.

"It was nice meeting you, Joely," Holt's father said. "Mike's told me a lot about you."

"He has?" she said, shooting Mike a confused look. Sure, they had worked together a Palekaiko, but she didn't know why Mike would be talking about her with his father.

"Don't talk to her," Holt said, pushing him inside the car. He turned back to her. "Get some sleep. I'll call you later."

"Okay." Joely blinked at him, watching all her plans to get to Palekaiko drive down the road. "Damn it."

"Aren't you going to get on the horse?" Mike said, already on top of his.

"I'm going to need some help getting in the saddle."

Rolling his eyes, Mike hopped off his horse and tried to boost her up. He didn't have his brother's strength, but thankfully the horse was patient. It wasn't pretty or graceful, but she managed to get into the saddle with a few bruises to her pride.

Mike, she noted jealously, vaulted back on to his horse like he did it every day.

"Why did you talk to your dad about me?" she asked them, as they rode down the long dusty driveway.

"Because you're Holt's girl. He was happy that Holt found someone. I told him all about you."

She blushed. "Why do you think I'm Holt's girl?"

"You're here with him, aren't you?"

116

Joely didn't want to get into the whole story with him, and besides it felt good to be called Holt's girl. "Why is your dad going to Palekaiko?"

"He needs a job." Mike shrugged. "Uncle Tetsuo won't let him work here, so he's going to try and get his old job back. I think Dude will hire him."

"What did he used to do?"

"Everything. But he's good at being a janitor. He knows how to clean the pool. He's a real pro at that. He didn't like working the front desk or dealing with people. He's shy, I guess. Not like me." He flashed her a grin.

"Where have you been?" She shifted in her saddle, trying to get comfortable. She needed more practice if she was going to be spending more time Upcountry. "I haven't seen you since you left the resort."

"I've been helping my dad. I liked Palekaiko, so maybe if he gets this job, I can go back to my old job too. It'll be just like old times."

Joely nodded, remembering Holt's words. "You know, Mike, your dad is an adult. He doesn't need his sons to take care of him."

Mike snorted. "Yeah, he does. He's shit at being an adult. Holt will tell you he's shit at being a father, but he loves us. He does his best. It's not his fault that his best is shit."

That was a lot of shit. Joely sighed. "I wish Holt had taken me with him. I would have liked to go back to Palekaiko for the day."

"Sick of this place, huh?" Mike nodded. "It can get to you. Especially with that old bastard Joe on your ass every five minutes."

"I like Joe," she defended him. "He's sweet."

"Are we talking the same Joe?"

"He's always been nice to me."

"I'll bet. He always had a weakness for redheads."

"That's disgusting," she said.

"It's true. Anyway, if you want to go to Palekaiko, I can take you."

"I'm not up for a horse ride that long."

"Uncle Tetsuo should have his Jaguar here. I know where the keys are."

"Then why were you riding horses into town?"

"Because my father is a stubborn idiot, which is where Holt gets it from. He wouldn't ride in Tetsuo's car."

"But stealing his horses is okay?"

"Borrowing. And these guys are actually his."

"His?"

"Technically. His mare and stallion bred these two. Their sires are long gone, but they were good stock."

Joely wasn't sure about the logic behind that, but who was she to argue? When they got back to the barn, she helped brush the horses down and made sure they were fed and had plenty of water.

"Were you serious about the Jag?" she asked.

"You bet."

"Okay, but can we go around dinner time? I'm beat."

"Sure, as long as you don't tell Holt."

"Deal." She shook hands with him.

"Cool. I'm going to raid the fridge, take a shower and catch some Z's. My room is on the third floor."

"I know," she said. "Holt is staying there."

"I figured he'd be staying with you."

"It's complicated."

"It always is," Mike said.

And he didn't even know the half of it.

Joely was surprised when she didn't hear from Holt that afternoon. Her nerves were so bad that even as tired as she was, she slept fitfully. When it was time to go, she made sure she had everything she cared about with her stuffed in the backpack with her laptop. If she had to run, she'd leave nothing she cared about behind.

Except for Holt.

And her friends.

And the ocean.

And just her whole life.

She had been really happy at the Palekaiko Beach Resort. Sure, there were times when she didn't want to clean another toilet or listen to Cami bitch that Lou-Lou stole her tips. But she lived in paradise. She didn't have to grift for her parents' approval or be involved in any convoluted schemes to make ends meet. She worked hard. Got paid for it. And her time was her own.

Joely didn't want to begin all over again.

True to his word, Mike produced the keys and walked with her to a locked garage. Inside, there was not only a Jaguar, but a Mercedes and a Humvee.

Joely got into the Jaguar. "Are you sure your uncle won't get mad that you're taking his car?"

"Mad? He'd lose his freakin' mind." Mike put the car into gear and tore down the driveway way too fast.

She fumbled with her seatbelt. "Slow down."

"What's the point in driving a sports car if you're not prepared to open her up?"

"Why aren't you working here at the ranch?" she asked.

Mike scowled. "Same reason as Holt. Uncle Tetsuo kicked us out. We're not coming back."

"That was a long time ago. I think he's had a change of heart."

"Not towards our dad."

"No, probably not," she admitted.

"I wanted a job with him. But not in this shit hole." He gestured to the ranch as they pulled out onto the highway.

"What's wrong with Hojo Ranch?"

"This is Holt's idea of paradise, not mine."

"It is?" Joely craned her head to look back at the ranch, but the dust the car was kicking up didn't give her a good view.

"Not me. I like sleeping late and spending the day in the ocean looking at pretty women. Holt likes getting up before the ass crack of dawn and smelling like cow shit."

Smirking, Joely checked her phone. It was almost five. By the time that they got to Palekaiko, Timothy would be at dinner. Hopefully.

"I wanted to work in Uncle Tetsuo's other organization." Mike looked over at her meaningfully.

"You wanted to be a gangster?" she ventured.

"You bet." He made a pistol out of his finger and thumb and cocked it at her. "But Uncle doesn't think I have the temperament for it. Holt, on the other hand, is his dream employee." Mike made a face. "But the joke is on Uncle Tetsuo. Holt hates his business. Blames it for our dad's drinking and breaking up our family and home. He was going to become a cop. But Uncle tried to buy Holt's way onto the force. So even though Holt passed all the exams, he decided to go into private security instead. But you know all of that."

She hadn't, but it was good to know.

"Can you put in a good word with Amelia about my dad? He's sober. He needs a job, especially one as sweet as the Palekaiko gig. Where else is he going to get room and board?"

"Yeah, I'll see what I can do," she said. "I've got to do a few things first. Can you wait for me, and take me back to the ranch afterwards?"

"Sure. I'm going to have to drop you off, though. I can't risk anyone recognizing the car. Uncle has eyes everywhere on that place."

"Don't you think that's kind of creepy?"

"He's obsessed with getting it back."

"He's not going to. Dude and Marcus will never sell."

"I know that. And you know that. But try telling that to Uncle."

When they got to the Palekaiko about an hour later, Mike dropped her off in the staff parking lot.

"Give me a call when you want me to pick you up. I'll be at a friend's house."

"Thanks," she whispered. She didn't see anyone she recognized, but she kept her head down anyway as she got out of the care.

Mike tore out of the parking lot, blaring the radio. Joely hurried to her room, looking furtively around her. Her fingers fumbled with her keys, but she finally got them to work in the lock and she pushed her way in. Closing the door and locking it behind her, she didn't dare turn on a light.

"Holt?" she said, hoping he wasn't there. She was in luck.

She walked around the small room, but it looked exactly how she left it, including a dirty towel that she had dropped on the floor. Out of habit, she picked it up and tossed it in the hamper. Sitting on the edge of her bed, she let out a large sigh that was mostly nerves.

Joely knew she couldn't afford to waste time. Still, it was hard to move. She made her first call to the Sunset restaurant.

Her hands were trembling, but she forced a bright perky tone into her voice when the call was answered on the first ring. "Aloha, I'm Marjorie Pierson with Go Go Hawaii. One of our contest winners, Timothy Andrews, won a hundred-dollar gift certificate for tonight. I'm just calling to confirm that he made it to the restaurant. We have a six o'clock reservation?"

Joely waited while the hostess checked.

"Yes," the hostess said. "The Senator's party has been seated."

"Excellent. Thanks for checking."

Joely let out a shaky sigh as she hung up. Then she texted Holt.

R U OK?

When he didn't answer, she got a little worried. But she figured he had his own problems to deal with. Stuffing a few more things that she had wanted to take with her into her backpack, Joely took a final look around.

"This isn't goodbye," she whispered.

But there was a part of her that thought it might be. If Timothy caught her, he'd kill her this time. She was as sure of that as she was of anything.

Feeling full of dread, she quickly changed into her maid's uniform and grabbed her copy of the master keys. In case anyone looked too closely at her, she didn't want them to see her backpack, so she grabbed a handful of towels. No one would think twice about a maid carrying a bunch of towels. After hiding the backpack in the pile of towels she was carrying, Joely left her room, locking it up.

Heading towards the guest rooms, she stuck to the back of the buildings, hoping she didn't run into anyone. At this time of the evening, though, the staff that was on duty was preparing for the luau and the staff that was off duty was gone.

Right now, she'd be kicking back with drinks with Kai, Hani and Makoa at the Hilton or maybe chillin' with Amelia and Michaela.

All the more reason to do this. If Joely could keep track of Timothy, she'd be much safer.

She made it up to the fourth floor without being seen.

"Housekeeping," she tapped on this door, careful not to stand in front of the peephole. "Housekeeping," she said one last time, before unlocking the door.

"Miss?"

Joely froze.

But it hadn't come from Timothy's room. It was the one across the hall.

"Can I have some fresh towels?"

"Certainly," she said through numbed lips. Joely handed her two from the bottom of her pile, being careful not to let her see the backpack.

The woman went back into her room without a thank you, and Joely let out the breath she was holding. Hurrying into the room, she locked it behind her.

After a quick look around the room, she found his computer plugged in on the desk. Shaking her head at how easy this was going to be, she opened her backpack and got to work.

Joely took his laptop apart to add in the hardware she was going to need to get remote access. She also put in a chip that would log every keystroke he did, so she could read whatever he typed. It was a backup, in case she missed something when she was using her remote access to search his computer. As she worked, Joely's hands stopped shaking. When her nervousness fled, working like this became almost Zen.

She felt like she did after meditating, calm and victorious. And a little sleepy, but that could be the past few days catching up on her. Joely felt like laughing, the relief was so strong.

This would help her from not becoming Timothy's victim. She would be in charge, now.

After rebooting, she checked the wireless connection and was able to duplicate the laptop's interface on an app she had wrote for her phone. With just a few flicks of her fingers, she could check Timothy's mail and call up any document or spreadsheet he was working on.

While the laptop ran its diagnostics, Joely wanted to make the trackers almost unidentifiable. It would suck if all her hard work went away once he ran a virus scan.

Joely read through his email and looked at his schedule while the computer processed her changes. Timothy had plans with "C" tomorrow to go snuba diving out of Maalaea Harbor. That would keep him busy while she met with her sister in Makawao.

The knots in her stomach started to slowly unravel. He also had to be back in the Minnesota state senate for a meeting in ten days.

Joely closed her eyes in relief. It was finally going to be over. She just had to go back to the ranch and enjoy the rest of her working vacation. And enjoy her security chief turned cowboy. How hot was that?

She was still smiling when she was putting the laptop back to where she found it when an email popped up.

You're late with the monthly payment. Send double by the tenth or copies of the bribes you took get sent to the press.

Joely's jaw dropped. Timothy was being blackmailed. She glanced at the clock. She'd been here an hour and she really should get going, but she needed to know more.

The fact that Timothy was taking bribes wasn't a shock to her. When he found out she knew about them was what caused him to beat her up so badly she had to be hospitalized. Joely had hacked into his computer back then too. He accepted campaign funds in exchange for doing favors for people. She had found the truth and was going to use it to leverage him into giving her a quick and quiet divorce.

Joely had hoped in five years he would have cleaned up his act, but apparently not. She went to work on the email address and searched for all the instances it appeared on his computer. Through a series of starts and stops, Joely finally found a locked file. She copied it onto a thumb drive to work on later. She had almost tracked where the person who was blackmailing Timothy was emailing from, when she heard the elevator ding.

Glancing wildly at the clock, she was shocked to see that an hour and a half had passed since the last time she looked.

Idiot!

"Fuck," she said, as she heard a man's voice and a high-pitched giggle.

The key fumbled. Thank God, the resort hadn't gotten the electronic keys yet on this floor. Joely did a hard reboot of the laptop, and stuffed her things into her backpack. She closed the top of the laptop. As the door opened, Joely dove out the sliding doors to the lanai and quietly pulled the door shut.

Her nerves and stomachache came back tenfold as she peeked through the gap of the drapes and saw Timothy come in with … Cami? That must have been who the C was. Oh gross! He was kissing her. They were ripping each other's clothes off. Joely dry heaved and leaned over the railing for air. She was a long way off the ground.

Maybe she could wait until they were asleep and then crawl into the room and out the door. She heard the bed springs start to squeak and the headboard slam against the wall.

This was not happening.

She wasn't jealous. That emotion was long since dead. It was disgust, pure and simple. When the moans and Cami's high pitched screams hit her ear, that was when Joely had enough. Slinging her foot over the railing, she was going to jump. It was going to hurt, but hopefully the plumeria bush would break her fall.

Her phone buzzed. Luckily it was on silent mode, even though with the racket going on inside, Joely doubted they could have heard her.

It was a text from Holt.

What the fuck are you doing?

I'm a little busy right now, she texted back.

I can see that.

Joely paused. That was a figure of speech, right?

Can you?

A flashlight beam caught her straddling the railing and she could just make out Holt standing there.

I sent Hani out for a ladder. Don't you fucking jump.

I can explain.

You bet your ass you will.

On a scale of 1-10 how in trouble am I?

11

Just 11?

Holt didn't answer. Hani was there minutes later with Kai and Makoa in tow, carrying the ladder. They swung the ladder around, narrowly missing Holt, who had to jump back to avoid getting smacked with it.

Great. It was Hawaii's answer to the Three Stooges.

She risked a peek into the room. Cami was happily riding on top of her ex. There was not enough eye bleach in the world for that. But it meant that both of them were too distracted to consider stopping what they were doing to investigate any strange sounds on the lanai.

When the ladder was set up and secure, Joely climbed down it as fast as she dared. Holt grabbed her upper arm in a vice grip.

"Thanks guys," she said.

They wouldn't look at her. She was in real trouble.

Holt marched her into his office. Flipping on his lights, he locked the door behind him.

"I'm not going to yell," he said in a calm voice.

"That's good," she said, sinking into a chair. She held her face in her hands.

He pulled up a chair across from her. "What the ever-loving fuck where you doing in his room?"

Joely thought about lying. She really did. Swallowing hard, she lifted her head to give him a line of bullshit. But then her eyes met his. She saw the worry, the concern, the hurt in them and whatever she planned to say flew out the window instead of out of her mouth.

"I hacked into his laptop to give me remote access."

Holt closed his eyes.

It didn't sound good when said aloud.

"I needed to know what he knew and where he would be. He's going back home as planned. At least, that's what his schedule said."

"You broke into a guest's hotel room, violated his privacy, and committed an illegal act."

Yeah that definitely didn't sound good when you said it aloud.

"I did it to protect myself."

"And that's why I'm not calling the police right now."

Joely jerked up straight in her chair. "The police? You'd have me arrested?"

Of course, he would. This was Holt they were talking about. Here they were again. She in her maid's outfit, and he in his security chief uniform. Why did she think this would end any different? Of course, this time she actually was guilty of what he was accusing her of.

"I need to confiscate your laptop though."

She thought about protesting. But she had her phone and the thumb drive. Holt just assumed that she would need her laptop to make use of what she did.

So, she meekly nodded and handed it over. If that was all it took to make things right, she'd gladly give him the computer.

"I'm so disappointed in you."

"Holt," she began, but he cut her off.

"I have no choice but to fire you."

Joely blinked at him. Was this the same man who hours ago, fingered her to an orgasm before a beautiful sunrise. "What?"

"I need your keys."

With nerveless fingers, she handed them over.

"I know our situation is unique."

"You think?" she said tartly.

"But I'll have your things boxed up and sent to the ranch for the time being. We can figure out where to go from there."

"That won't be necessary," she said, standing up. "Donate them."

"Joely, I have no choice but to fire you."

"I understand. You're just doing your job." She did understand. This was Holt. This had always been Holt. Joely had no reason to feel betrayed or hurt. She'd known what type of man Holt was. She'd know what type of woman she was. She had known that they would never work out. She was an idiot to have cultivated any small hope that they would make it.

"You can still stay at the ranch. Until you've made other plans."

"I've made other plans." She went to the door and opened it.

"When?" he asked.

"Just now." She closed the door behind her. Joely walked slowly, hoping that Holt would fling open the door and ask her to wait.

He didn't.

She knew he wouldn't.

She took out her phone and called his brother. "Hi Mike. I need you to come pick me up. And I need to borrow your yurt."

Chapter Fourteen

Mike met her at Whaler's Village, which was an eerie similarity to how this all started. After explaining everything that happened over the past week, Joely had to beg Mike not to turn the car around so he could "kick his brother's ass."

"It's okay," she said.

"It's not okay."

But in the end Joely managed to convince him to drive her back towards Makawao. She needed to meet with her sister more than ever now.

"You want to go back to the ranch?"

"No, I can't run the risk of running into Holt. I was thinking of camping out at Baldwin Beach."

"No," Mike said. "It's not safe there. Too many tweakers and meth heads at night. But the waves are choice during the day."

"Hookipa?" she asked.

"Nah, the rangers get a stick up their butt. It's illegal." Mike took his hands off the wheel to do finger quotes around the word illegal.

That was the story of her life in one gesture. "I need to go to the street festival tomorrow. I'm meeting my sister there."

Mike arched an eyebrow at her. "Is she cute?"

Joely had to smile. "I haven't seen her in a while, but yeah, she's cute."

"Is she single?" He waggled his eyebrows.

"Mike," she warned.

"Why don't you call Amelia or Michaela? They can put you up for the night."

Joely shook her head. "I'm too ashamed. I couldn't bear it if they were disappointed in me."

"Holt's got a stick up his ass too. I should take you to Uncle Tetsuo's place in Wailea."

"No, don't. You'll get in trouble for taking his car."

"Yeah, you're right. Still, I can't have you camping out all alone. You can crash at my friend's BnB. It's right by Baby Beach, the one off Baldwin Beach, not the one down in Lahaina. It's empty because it's basically a shed and the last people who booked it trashed her on the internet. If you can leave her a good review on Yelp, she'll call it even."

"Deal," Joely said, getting out her phone.

"And in the morning, we can do some surfing at Hookipa if you're feeling up to it. If not, we can do Baldwin."

Joely was going to refuse. The waves on the North Shore were no joke. Professional surfers drowned there, especially the ones who went way out to Peahi to surf Jaws. But if this was her last time on Maui to surf, there wasn't a better spot than the North Shore beaches. "Your friend got a board?"

"Roger dat."

"Shoots," she said.

"Radical." Mike fist bumped her.

About an hour later, they headed into a residential area and he pulled into a driveway. Lights were on in the main house.

"Stay here for a minute."

Joely wanted out of her maid's uniform in the worst way. At this point, she'd be willing to sleep in the car as long as Mike drove it far away from Holt.

After a few minutes, he came back with a triumphant shaka. "You can stay."

"Thanks." She gathered her things and got out of the car. He led her around to the back yard, a dog barked from inside and Joely could hear the noise of a television showing a sitcom.

Mike hadn't been kidding. It was a shed. But it had a twin bed inside and a working sink and toilet.

"It's got no frills, but she makes bank on the surfers in January."

"It's perfect," she said.

"Bolt the door after I leave, and no one should bother you. But you got your phone, just in case?"

Joely nodded. "Thanks for this, Mike."

He shuffled his feet. "Do you want me to talk to Holt? Smooth things over?"

She shook her head. "I think we've lied enough. It's time to make things a reality. I'm leaving with my sister. My ex won't find me."

"I don't want you to go," he said, and gave her a quick hug.

"Don't make me cry," she begged.

He wiped his nose on his jacket sleeve. "We'll talk about this in the morning. Can I get you anything?"

"Just the surfboard tomorrow."

"It's going to work out," Mike said, not realizing he was saying the same thing his brother had said to her.

She tried for a smile.

"Get some sleep," he said.

Even though she was exhausted, Joely knew that she wouldn't be able to sleep. After bolting the door, she tried to charge her phone. The first outlet was dead, but she caught a break on the one by the toilet. Reaction started to set in and she knew if she started to cry, she wouldn't stop. So, she found some cleaning supplies and went to work.

Two hours later, she had to walk outside to get away from the chemical smells. But she'd bet money that was the cleanest that shed had ever been.

She could hear the ocean from here. Leaning up against a tree, she let the soft night air caress her. If she hugged the tree and pretended it was Holt, Joely didn't begrudge herself the fantasy.

A while later, she heard some whoops and raucous laughter. She wasn't in the mood to party or deal with people, so she locked herself inside the shed. The harsh smell had dissipated. She was grateful for the clean sheets that smelled faintly like bleach, and she rolled over to check the charge on her phone.

No calls from Holt.

It hurt.

More than she liked. But what else could they say to each other than hadn't already been said.

She checked the activity on Timothy's laptop, but it hadn't been touched at all. After witnessing the bedroom gymnastics, she was pretty sure checking his email was last on his list for tonight. What would he do when he saw the blackmail message?

Joely wondered about the blackmailer's identity. If she knew Holt was going to react the way he had, she wouldn't have given up her laptop so easily. She could have spent the night trying to crack open that folder or tracking down the email that the blackmailer used.

Oh well, the blackmailer's identity could wait until she was safely off the island.

Turning off the bare bulb light, Joely was grateful for a soft bed, and if the water leaking out of her eyes wet the pillow, well it should be dry in the morning.

***

It was ironic that the first time on her vacation she got to sleep late she was in a shed. Mike woke her up at eleven, banging on the door. He brought some doughnuts on a stick for her and a large coffee for breakfast.

She kicked him out afterwards so she could change into her bathing suit. She considered the ridiculous purple bikini, but it would be just her luck to have a wave rip it off her. So, she went for her Billabong one piece. It was black with neon pink stripes on the side. She always felt like a bad ass when she was wearing it.

"What's it gonna be, wahine? Baldwin or Hookipa?"

"Hookipa," she said. "Fuck it." If the locals gave her attitude, she'd give it right back. All she wanted was one great wave to remember and they could have the rest. "Has your uncle noticed his car is missing?"

"Nah, he's got his own problems."

"Where did you stay last night?"

"Up in my room at the ranch."

Joely swore that she wasn't going to ask about Holt, but after a few minutes her will broke down. "Was Holt there?"

135

"Nah, Pops said he's spitting nails at Palekaiko."

Joely thought for a moment and then simply said, "Good." Why should she be the only one suffering?

"Yeah good as long as you're not in his way."

"Where are our boards?" she asked as she put on sunscreen and braided her hair tight to her scalp.

"They'll be at the beach. We're meeting friends."

Joely hoped it was the BnB owner. She wanted to thank them personally. It had been nice to be alone and feel safe. It was even nicer to sleep until lunch time. "Is there going to be a cook out?"

"Do I look like an amateur?"

Joely made a mental list of everything she hoped was at the picnic. She refused to be sad. This was her goodbye to Maui party, but it was going to be a celebration.

They parked at Hookipa and walked towards the pavilion. She saw Makoa first.

"Oh no. We can't stay here."

Then she heard Amelia laugh. Dude was grilling hot dogs on a hibachi. "I don't think that's allowed," Joely whispered, looking over her shoulder.

"He's a billionaire. He paid good money for the rangers to look the other way."

Out in the ocean, she saw Michaela in the lineup and Marcus riding a wave in. As they got closer, she got a lump in her throat. They had brought her board and it was jammed in the sand with the rest of the crew's boards, just like always. Her long board was neon pink with a stencil of a turtle in black. Kai had hand painted it for her. She thought she would never see it again. Running her hand over it, she wished she could take it with her.

Hani and Kai saw them first and hurried over. If they were mean to her, she was going to lose it. Panic set in and she braced to run. But Hani caught her in a hug and whirled her around.

"We missed you."

Now, she really was bawling. Kai was next. And he took off his shirt to dry her eyes. "Stop that shit. If Makoa sees you crying, he'll start to cry too."

She sniffed and gave a watery giggle.

"Don't blow snot on my shirt," Kai said.

"I'm not." She threw it back at him.

Makoa let out a whoop when he saw her and grabbed her.

"What?" she managed to get out before he slung her over his shoulder. Grabbing his board, he ran into the ocean with her.

"We're gonna go tandem," he said.

"Here?" she screeched. "Are you crazy?"

"Sometimes. Help me paddle."

It wasn't like he was giving her much choice in the matter.

Kneeling on the board, they paddled out, passing Michaela who was riding a wave in.

"You guys don't hate me?" Joely asked when Michaela smiled and gave her the shaka.

"Of course not. We could never hate you."

She swallowed hard. "Holt does."

"Nah, he's just thick headed."

"Is he here?"

"Sistah, who do you think is running the place if we're all here?"

137

"Who?" she said, as they got in the surfing line-up to wait their turn for a wave.

"Holt and his daddy. If you thought Holt was in a bad mood last night, you wouldn't want to see him today."

Joely pressed her forehead against Makoa's wide back. "I don't think that's in the cards."

"You never know. Ask Zarafina."

"Is she here too?"

"No, she stayed back. I think she's got a crush on Mel. That's Holt's daddy."

It was glorious to float in the ocean. Joely crushed the part of her that kept looking for Holt and when it was their turn for the wave, she almost lost her nerve.

"Keep kneeling on the board and wait until I'm about to pop. Then crawl on my shoulders."

"You're nuts."

"Just do it. We got this."

Yeah, we didn't.

Not the first time.

Or the second.

But the third time, they made it back to shore and the whole beach erupted in applause. Of course, by that time Joely's hair was a sodden mess all over her face and she was shaky from laughing and swallowing all that salt water.

But they missed the rocks and the coral.

"I think we deserve a hot dog."

"Roger dat," Makoa said, high fiving her.

"That was awesome! I've got it all on my camera." Amelia gave her a hug. Joely hung on to her.

"I'm so so sorry."

"You're not fired," Amelia said.

"But Holt…"

"Doesn't have a say in the matter." Amelia dusted her hands off as if that ended the matter. And for Amelia, it probably did.

"Is Dude pissed at me?"

"Dude doesn't get pissed." They walked over to the cooler. Amelia cracked open a beer and handed her one.

Joely tanked half of it, which she probably shouldn't have done with only doughnuts and a cup of coffee in her stomach, but damn she needed it.

"What about Marcus?"

"What about him?" Michaela said, coming up for her hug.

"I guess he's disappointed in me too."

"He might have been if Holt got to him first with his side of the story." Michaela laughed. "Luckily, Mike called last night and told us everything."

"Everything?" Joely winced.

"Yeah." She punched her lightly on the arm. "You should have called me. You could have been spending the last week on a yacht instead of a cattle ranch."

"The cattle ranch was kind of fun. And I didn't want to intrude. This whole situation is so fucked up."

"Honey, you hid me from Holt while I squatted in the hotel. I owe you. And you are so not fired," Michaela said.

"See?" Amelia handed Michaela a beer.

"What's Holt going to say?" Joely finished her beer and accepted a hot dog from Dude.

"What he always does. But it'll die down and things will get back to normal." Amelia hooked her arm through her husband's. "Right?"

"Shoots," he said. "Want to go tandem?"

"No, I'd rather not drown," Amelia said.

"Then let's go fool around in the car."

Amelia thought about it, and then shrugged. "Shit, why not? I haven't had a day off in ages. Do you think I should check in on Holt first?"

"No," was the consensus of everyone else.

Joely declined to answer.

"Anyway, Marcus will have the yacht meet you at Malikeo Bay tonight. And you can stay aboard until Timothy flies back home."

"This can't be real." Joely's head was spinning.

"You'll be saying there tonight. The chef is cooking up lobster thermidor and chocolate mousse."

Oddly, Joely wondered what the ranch hands were going to eat tonight. She had been planning on making clam chowder and serving it in bread bowls.

"Thank you," she said simply. "I can't thank you enough."

"Girlfriend, I would have done the same thing," Michaela said.

"But I broke the law and the resort's rules."

Amelia shrugged. "What some tight asses don't get is that the rules are guidelines. Sometimes rules should be broken. In this case, Timothy is a powerful and dangerous man who already put you in the hospital once. He got away with that. Never again."

Joely had a hard time swallowing her hot dog. All she ever wanted was to have Holt say something like that, but all he saw was black and white. She shook herself out of the funk that was threatening to come over her. There was no sense wishing a tiger would change his stripes. They had a dream of a week together, with the sweetness of possibility making it all that more poignant. She wouldn't ruin those memories with regret.

And who knows, maybe it would all work out.

After Timothy left and she went back to her job at the resort, things would be awkward for a while. But Holt had always been her friend. She was sure that even if they lost the great sex and connection they had on the ranch, he would eventually get over this.

And if he didn't, there was always the new identity her sister was going to give her tonight.

Chapter Fifteen

Holt was being punished. He knew when Kai, Hani, and Makoa all came down with the flu that he was in for a bad day. But then Amelia also called in sick, and Marcus and Dude were nowhere in sight. Michaela wasn't answering his calls. Holt was the highest-ranking employee here, and he was having to make do with the second shift after promising them overtime, just to keep the resort running smoothly.

He was tempted to call Joely. Hell, if he was being honest with himself, he wanted to call her all night.

He missed her.

And he couldn't shake the feeling that he did the wrong thing. But how could following the rules be wrong? Sure, Senator Andrews was a first-class shit, but Joely didn't need to sink to his level. Their plan had been working.

Did she not have enough faith in him? Holt had promised to keep her safe. Did she not believe him? When he saw her up on that balcony, his life flashed before his eyes. If Timothy pushed her or if she jumped, Holt couldn't have gotten there in time.

The switchboard buzzed. He had Cami handling the guest's requests. He was doing concierge and his father and Zarafina were doing the bus boys' jobs. He had a splitting head ache and an even deeper appreciation of what Amelia did all day.

"Palekaiko Beach Resort," he said, looking down at phone's display to see who was calling. It was room 418. Holt froze, feeling an unfamiliar flash of emotion. Hatred. If it wasn't for this man, everything would have been normal.

142

Of course, Holt and Joely would have probably gone on not connecting. If anything, he should be grateful for Timothy Andrews for pushing them together.

Holt needed to call Joely. He had been a huge idiot. He'd ask Marcus to consider hiring her back. Holt would take full responsibility for her actions. Then he'd beg her to come back. He wouldn't blame her if she didn't want anything further to do with him, but he would make this right.

He had just been so angry yesterday, still reeling from his father forcing his way back into his life.

"Hello?" Timothy said, impatiently.

Holt hadn't heard a damn word he just said. "Uh, sorry. Our phone lines are having technical difficulties." He rolled his eyes at his own lame excuse. "Can you repeat?"

"I said, I'm expecting a visitor. Please escort him immediately to my room."

"Sure." Holt was suspicious. Could Timothy have hired a private investigator? Did he know where Joely was? "What's your visitor's name?"

"Tetsuo Hojo."

"I'm sorry?" Holt almost dropped the phone.

Timothy spelled the name, slowly and loudly. "Did you get that?"

"Yeah, I got it." Holt hung up.

His father shot him a questioning look.

"You better take care of some of the janitorial duties. Go check the pool's PH or something."

"I already did, and the customers are more important."

"Since when?" Holt said, trying to control his sneer.

"Since I got sober."

He didn't have an answer for that.

"Where's your girl?" Mel crossed his arms and leaned against a pillar in the lobby.

"She's not my girl."

"You fucked it up already? Shame. I would have liked to have gotten to know her."

Gritting his teeth, Holt managed to hold on to his temper.

"How's your mother?"

"Fine. Look, why don't you take an early lunch? We're going to get hit pretty hard this afternoon."

"Zarafina is on break. I'll wait until she gets back. Why do I get the feeling you're trying to get rid of me?"

"Because he is." Tetsuo glided into the lobby with two of his goons behind him.

"What's your business with Timothy Andrews?" Holt barked.

"Come with me and see. In the meantime, make yourself useful, Mel. Man the desk until Holt gets back. Do you think you can handle that?"

If his father was intimidated by Tetsuo in his three-piece suit looking slick and confident, while Mel was in a bell boy uniform, he didn't show it.

"Not a problem," Mel drawled.

Holt hid a smirk when he saw that answer go right up his uncle's nose. He fell in step next to his uncle, after giving his two bodyguards the side eyes.

"So, what's up?"

144

"Senator Andrews has been asking a lot of questions about you and your friend."

"Like what?"

"Like offering a bounty on your heads." Tetsuo's face was grim.

"He's offering money for someone to kill Joely?" Rage blinded Holt for a moment and he stopped in his tracks. Would Joely have had warning of this if Holt hadn't taken away her computer? It was still locked up in his office. He'd bring it back to her and apologize.

"Kidnap rather than kill. Apparently, he wants something from her first. I thought it was only fair to see what the senator was willing to pay five thousand dollars for. And to discourage him from wasting money on trying to kidnap my nephew."

"And Joely."

Tetsuo shrugged. "You are no longer together. She is not my concern anymore."

"She's my concern."

"Really? Then where is she?"

Holt didn't have an answer for him, and probably wouldn't tell him if he did. Instead, he ignored the question. "What's going to happen when we get to the room?"

"That depends on how reasonable the senator is willing to be."

Holt led them up to room 418 and knocked.

The door flung open. "You!" Timothy said, his fists clenching.

Tetsuo flicked a finger in his direction and his two goons pushed Timothy back into the room. Tetsuo followed at a more reasonable pace. Holt locked the door behind them.

145

"What is the meaning of this?" Timothy blustered.

"We're here for the bounty. I've brought you the man you've been inquiring about. Where's my money?"

Timothy went to the safe in the room and pulled out a wad of hundreds. Holt watched his uncle count fifty bills before pocketing it.

"Ask your questions."

"Get out," Timothy said.

"No." Tetsuo settled into the desk chair, his body guards taking position behind him.

Timothy opened his mouth to protest, but decided against it. He whirled to Holt. "Where's my wife?"

"I don't know."

"You're a fool for protecting her," Timothy said. "She's not Miss Sweet and Innocent. She comes from a family of grifters and murderers."

"Then why are you stalking your *ex*-wife." Holt put a big emphasis on the word ex. "I would imagine you'd be glad to get rid of her."

"Because she's been bleeding me dry for five years and it has to end."

Holt flicked a glance to his uncle, but his face was unreadable. "What are you talking about?"

"You didn't know?" Timothy peered into Holt's eyes. Holt didn't like him. He had a rat's face and beady eyes. "Oh, that's rich. She's probably conning you too. How much money have you given her?"

"What do you mean bleeding you dry?" Tetsuo asked, while Holt frowned in confusion.

146

Timothy whirled back to him. "She's been blackmailing me. Five thousand a month for the last five years."

"Why didn't you go to the police?" Holt asked.

Tetsuo rolled his eyes.

"Because if it was something I wanted the police to be involved in, there would be no need to blackmail me," Timothy snarled.

"Was it the fact that you beat the shit out of her and put her in the hospital?"

"No."

Tetsuo frowned. Holt knew that for all of his uncle's reputation, he didn't like violence against women.

"What are you planning to do if you find Joely?"

"Who?"

Holt grimaced. "Annie. Your ex-wife."

"That little bitch is a hacker."

"Watch your mouth," Holt warned him.

"All I want is her fucking computer with the data she has against me and all the copies. If I get that, I'll be happy to never see her again. If she holds out on me and starts the blackmailing shit up again." Timothy shrugged. "I'll never stop hunting her."

Looking up at the ceiling, Holt debated what to do. "Let me get this straight. You get the computer, all copies of the data, and you'll go back to Minnesota and never try to contact her again. You won't try to kidnap her or hurt her."

"She means less than nothing to me. She's trash. Her family is trash. I'd love it if she drowned or met another unfortunate accident."

Holt stepped forward, with his fists clenched. Tetsuo's goons moved to block him.

"Really?" he said to his uncle.

Tetsuo rose from his chair. "Senator Andrews, if you get the information you are seeking, will you never return to Maui again?"

"Sure."

"And you won't seek retribution against Joely, err I mean Annie," Holt added, shrugging off the goons.

Timothy sighed. "Fine. Whatever." Everyone in the room stared at him expectantly. "Yes. I won't care if the bitch lives or dies."

Tetsuo cocked his head at Holt.

"I can get you the laptop. It's in my office. And I can probably convince her to give me the copies."

"All the copies," Timothy said.

Holt nodded.

"Then I think we have an agreement."

"I'll be right back." Holt left Tetsuo and Timothy in the room together and hurried down to his office.

On the way, he texted Joely.

I need to see you.

He wasn't surprised that there wasn't any answer.

Timothy put a bounty on our heads. Tetsuo and I just talked to him. He said if you give him all the copies, he'll go back to MN and this all ends.

Holt unlocked his file cabinet and took out the laptop. His phone buzzed and he looked down.

I have no idea what you're talking about.

Joely, please, he texted back. *You can end this by just stopping what you're doing and giving up on your revenge.*

You're a crackpot. Stay away from me. And stay away from Timothy.

"Stubborn," he muttered, and took his frustration out on the stairs going up to the fourth floor.

Not bothering to knock, Holt pushed his way into the room and handed the computer over to Timothy.

"What's this?" Timothy said, turning it over and over.

"Her computer."

"What are you trying to pull? Is this where she keeps the copies? Because I need her laptop. It's got this stupid fucking picture of an alien's head on it." Timothy smashed the computer on the ground and jumped on it. "You've got twenty-four hours before I resume my search. Mr. Hojo has explained to me that you're not involved, so my beef isn't with you. But if I don't have the data I need by Sunday morning, I'm going to have her killed."

Holt reacted. The goons were too slow. He kicked out, popping Timothy's knee out of joint. As Timothy screamed on the way down, Holt whirled in a round house kick that whipped Timothy's head to the side. He was unconscious on the ground before anyone moved.

Tetsuo slow clapped. "It's about time, boy. Go get your girl. I can use someone with her skills. We'll clean up in here."

"No," Holt said, his breathing ragged. "Get out. Leave him to me."

"You can't let him live. He'll press assault charges."

149

Holt shook his head. "No, he won't. He'd be too worried about what I would say to the police."

"You've made an enemy of him." Tetsuo stepped over the body. "It's not wise to let people like that live."

"I'm not a murderer."

"Which is why I said I would take care of it."

"I don't need your help."

Now, it was Tetsuo's turn to shake his head. "Then you better find your girl before he does."

Chapter Sixteen

Joely was sunburned, and still a little tipsy when Mike dropped her off on Baldwin Street, while he found a place to park.

The street festival was in full party mode with the road blocked off on either end. Food trucks lined the sides, and there was a crowd of people that Joely slipped in and out of, while looking for her sister. She was still a little buzzed from the beer, the sun, and the waves. If things didn't work out, perhaps she could go to Tahiti or Australia. She liked island life.

A local band had set up a make-shift bandstand and started to play covers of top forty songs. She grabbed a beer and danced along, keeping her buzz alive. Out of the corner of her eye, she saw a wide pair of shoulders and a nice butt. Joely watched him and he appeared to be alone. When her favorite song came on, it seemed perfectly natural to walk up to the muscled stranger and ask him to dance.

"Aloha," she said, putting her arm on his large bicep. "You wanna dance?"

The man turned and she nearly dropped her beer. "Holt," she squeaked when his arm came around her and pulled her in tight. "What are you doing here?"

He frowned at her. "You didn't know it was me? Why are you asking strange men to dance?"

She wasn't sure how to answer that and was equally unsure how to get out of his arms now that they were dancing to Zedd's *The Middle*, which seemed appropriate to the situation. So, she just went with it, singing and dancing along to the band.

151

When the song ended and the band went into *Meant to Be* by Bebe Rexha, Holt hugged her close. This time, she did drop her cup. It was a good thing it was empty. Laying her head on his chest, she closed her eyes and swayed with him. Just for this song, she would pretend that yesterday never happened.

Joely heard his heart beating over the noise of the crowd because it seemed the world had narrowed down to just the two of them.

This, she thought, blinking back tears. *I want this.*

So naturally, the next song was *Something Just Like This* by Coldplay and the Chainsmokers.

One more song, she promised herself. One more song to enjoy being held like she mattered. One more song to feel like she deserved to be loved.

Taking a deep breath, she smelled the lime soap he used and the crisp scent of his aftershave. She probably smelled like booze and salt water, but she didn't care. He didn't either, if the way he held her was any indication. This was another nice memory to add, if this was going to be her last day in Maui.

The band took a break from playing the soundtrack to her life, and Joely knew she should move out of Holt's arms. The fuck of it was she just didn't want to. But people jostled them and she needed to find her sister, so she stepped back first.

"That was nice," she said. "See ya."

She shouldn't have expected to get away so easily. It would have been a nicer memory to have rather than their confrontation last night.

When he leaned down, she froze. Was he going to kiss her? Closing her eyes, Joely parted her lips. But he moved to her ear and said in a low voice. "If you give me all the copies of the blackmail stuff, Timothy said he'll leave you alone for good."

Frustration made her sag and shove him. "I'm not the one blackmailing him. Not that you're going to fucking believe me anyway."

She successfully pulled out of his grip and darted through the crowd. Of course, he was following her this time when she didn't want him too.

"Joely, wait."

She got in line at the empanada truck. If she was going to have to deal with Holt, she was going to make him buy her dinner. Turning her back on him, she stared at the menu.

Did she want the Hana which was chicken, onions, peppers, mushrooms, and asparagus, or did she want the Hookipa which had beef, onions, peppers, olives, onions, and a boiled egg?

Both.

And she was getting a lilikoi shave ice for dessert.

"I'm sorry," he said when he caught up to her. "I was wrong."

That hadn't been what she was expecting to hear. Had anyone in her life ever said that to her?

An older woman ahead of her in line, gave Holt an appreciative once over. "Sistah, when a man who looks like that is apologizing to you, you hear him out."

"Thank you, Auntie," Holt said, with a hand over his heart.

The older woman blushed. "And he's polite too."

"Five minutes?" Holt said. "And then if you want me to leave you alone, I will."

Joely looked down at her feet.

153

"It's just five minutes," the woman said. "I'll even hold your place in line."

Smiling, Joely looked around to see if she could see her sister. But she didn't see anyone who looked like her. "All right. I'll be back," she said to the woman.

"Honey, I hope not."

Holt slung his arm around Joely's shoulder and it felt too good for her to shake him off. He led her down the street away from the crowd until the only thing around them was a chicken who was hoping for a handout.

"What are you doing here?" she asked.

"I was on my way back to the ranch. They're counting on me to finish up the week. Of course, the road is closed until nine, so I decided to get some ono grindz and wish you were with me."

She crossed her arms over her chest, refusing to be charmed.

Remember, he had considered calling the cops on you.

"What are you doing here?" he asked.

"I'm meeting with someone."

"Who?"

"None of your business."

"Are you blackmailing Timothy?"

Joely sighed. "You're not going to believe me anyway, so why should I tell you."

"I'll believe you."

"You have never believed me," she said, holding herself tighter.

He sighed and looked over her head. "I know. It's because you've always made me a little suspicious. Like there was something you were hiding. Some secret you were protecting."

154

"Lots of them, actually," she said. "And there's more than what you know, so I think it's best that we just go back to being friends."

Still not looking at her, he nodded. "Sure. If that's what you want."

"Is it going to be a problem that the Kincaides have overruled you firing me?"

He gave a half laugh. "Where were you guys today?"

"Hookipa?"

Holt looked at her this time, with a big grin on his face. "How did you do."

She held up her arms triumphantly. "No scars. No blood."

"Proud of you."

Joely blinked back tears. Had anyone ever said that to her before?

"So, if you're not blackmailing your ex, who is?"

"That's a good question," she said. "Could be anyone. I was going to try and find out but you've got my computer."

He winced. "Yeah, not anymore. Timothy smashed it."

She shrugged. She'd wait until Timothy accessed his bank account and she would deduct the funds out of it once she set up an untraceable way to receive it.

"But he really wants your ALIENWARE computer."

Nostalgia hit her full force. "Oh man, me too. I loved that rig. When we were still married, he bought it for me. I gave him the exact specs and told him I needed it for college. It was a dream."

"Where is it now?"

155

"After he hit me in the head with it a couple of times, I went unconscious. I assumed he destroyed it."

A muscle worked in Holt's jaw. "I should have let Tetsuo take care of him."

She really didn't want to fall in love with Holt, but when he said things like that it was difficult not to. Her infatuation had turned to lust and was starting to get into the real emotions. That wouldn't be good for either of them.

Rubbing his arm, Joely said, "Thanks. But you don't want to get involved in crap like that. You're above it and that's how it should be."

"He thinks you still have that computer and have been using the contents to blackmail him five grand a month since you left."

Joely snorted. "Yeah, like if I had bank like that I'd be living at Palekaiko instead of busting my ass working there."

"That's what I thought," he nodded.

Narrowing her eyes at him, she said, "Wait. You believe me."

"Yes, I believe you. But I'm not the one that matters."

"You matter," she whispered.

He cupped her face and kissed her on the lips. It was short and sweet. Friends did that, right? "I meant that Timothy has to believe it."

"He won't."

"Shit."

"Why?"

Holt looked down at the ground. His fists clenched. "He said if he doesn't get the laptop by tomorrow, he's going to put a contract out on your life."

Joely sighed. So much for staying in Maui. "Figures."

"Is that all you have to say?" Holt glared up at her.

"What are you expecting from me? It's obvious now that I can't stay. This island will be the first place his contract killers are going to look. I guess you get your wish after all. Cami will make a good head housekeeper."

"No, she won't," Holt made a face.

"Thanks for that."

"You're coming back to the ranch with me."

"No, I'm not putting you guys in danger."

"You won't. Have you forgotten who owns the ranch?"

"No, I know exactly who and what is behind that ranch and I don't want you to get involved in organized crime, nor do I want to spend my life a prisoner there."

"It would be just until…"

"Just until what? Tetsuo kills him? Or worse, sends you to do it." She shook her head emphatically. "No, absolutely not. I won't allow it."

"Then what are you going to do?" he said, grabbing her by the upper arms.

She grabbed him back. "The less you know, the better."

"I can't accept that."

"You're going to have to. I'm not a wounded bird you can nurse back to health and keep in a cage."

"I don't want to cage you. Handcuff for a little while, maybe."

He surprised a laugh out of her. "No, we're just friends. No benefits."

157

"I think I could convince you."

Joely thought he could too.

"Hey, there you are!" Mike called out from behind her.

"Fuck off. We're having a conversation," Holt said.

"That's rude." Joely turned to Mike and stared. He had his arm around Sammy.

Sammy was dressed like a beach bunny with heart shaped sunglasses and a star-spangled bikini. A large tote bag hung off her shoulder. Joely wondered if her identity was in it.

She took a step towards them, but Sammy held out her hand. "Hi, I'm Samantha Kane. You must be Joely. Mike has told me so much about you."

Joely took her sister's hand and shook it. "Yeah, Mike talks about me a lot."

"You must be Holt," Samantha said, shaking his hand as well.

"How did you two meet?" Joely asked.

"He rents my BnB from time to time."

Joely opened her mouth, but Sammy cut her off again.

"It's never been so clean. Thank you."

"You live on the island?" Joely said, trying to keep her outrage out of her voice. Why didn't she contact her before now? Why did she let her stay in the shed instead of inviting her into her home?

"I wish. My job takes me all over the world."

Yeah, I guess it did.

"I rent a house to a nice family. You stayed in the shed on their property last night."

"You stayed in a shed last night? I told you to come back to the ranch."

"Do you think there might have been a reason I didn't want to go back to the ranch last night?" Joely asked.

"What do you do for a living?" Holt asked Sammy, filling in the awkward silence.

"I'm an expeditor for a worldwide construction company."

Good cover. Joely nodded.

"Well, it was nice to meet you. I'm sure you and Mike would like to be alone." Holt put his arm around Joely and walked backwards a few steps.

"Oh shit," Samantha said, looking over Joely's head.

"What?" Joely turned and saw Tetsuo and two large men walking towards them.

"Oh shit," Mike said.

"Yeah," Holt said. "That about sums it up."

Tetsuo was practically beaming when he came up to them.

"Samantha, welcome back to the island."

"Mr. Hojo," she said respectfully.

"I wasn't aware you knew my nephews."

"Your nephews?" she said, flinching away from Mike.

"Unc," Mike protested. "Why do you got to do shit like that?"

"I wasn't aware that these men were your nephews," Samantha said quickly.

"You know him?" Joely said, jerking her thumb at Tetsuo.

"I've utilized Ms. Kane's skills in the past."

"Huh," she said. That made sense. Small world.

"Why don't we get away from the crowds and go back to my ranch?" Tetsuo asked.

"The roads are closed until nine," Mike said.

"Not to me, they're not. Now, give your brother the keys to the Jaguar."

"You boosted the Jag?" Holt cried.

"It's not boosting if you have the keys," Mike grumbled digging in his pocket for them.

"It's boosting if you don't have permission," Tetsuo said mildly.

"I don't think Samantha and I should intrude on your family time." Joely resisted the urge to bow to Tetsuo. She would have jumped out into traffic, if there was any, to avoid going back to the ranch. She needed to get her sister alone so they could utilize her twenty-four-hour head start to the best of their abilities.

Tetsuo smiled. "I actually have business to discuss with Samantha, so it will be a mix of family time and business. Besides, the paniolos are disappointed that you didn't cook tonight."

"They were?" Joely said, feeling a pang of guilt.

"I'm sure all will be forgiven if you make those clam chowder bowls you promised."

"Do you know everything?" Joely asked.

Holt cleared his throat that sounded like a hidden laugh.

"Knowledge is power, my dear. The four of you take the Jag. Holt is driving," Tetsuo said loudly to stop any protest from Mike. "I'll have Alan drive your car up to the ranch." He snapped his fingers and one of the gentlemen behind him bowed and went in the direction of the parking lot.

160

Joely looked at Samantha who shrugged.

She shrugged back. Looks like they didn't have much of a choice. She left a message on Michaela's voice mail thanking her for the offer of the yacht, but she and Holt had made other plans. The Palekaiko gang would be happy about that. But she was really going to miss the lobster thermidor.

Chapter Seventeen

Holt loved driving the jaguar, but he really wished that it was just him and Joely. They had a lot to talk about, but at least he knew where she was going to sleep tonight and it wasn't going to be in a damned shed. If he could convince her to stay at the ranch until they figured out who was the blackmailer, she'd be safe.

True to Tetsuo's word, the barricades were removed to allow his sedan, Holt's Accord, and the Jaguar through before they were put back in place again.

"You guys all right back there?" Joely asked.

"It's a little cramped, but we'll survive," Samantha said.

Mike continued to sulk.

"Timothy's going to put a hit out on me," Joely said.

Holt jerked in his seat. Why the hell was she talking to them about this?

"That asshole," Mike said.

"You should get out of the country," Samantha said calmly.

"No, she shouldn't." That's all Holt needed was for Samantha to offer to take Joely to the mainland where he couldn't protect her. "She's safe here. If you worked with Tetsuo before, you know that."

Samantha leaned back in her seat. "He has a point."

Holt thought it was odd that Samantha didn't ask who Timothy was or why he wanted Joey dead. Unless Mike knew the whole story and had talked to her about it. That wouldn't surprise him because Mike couldn't keep his mouth shut.

"What are you going to do, Joely?" Mike asked.

"There's not much I can do. He thinks I've got something that I don't have, and he'll never believe me."

"Is Uncle going to handle it for you?"

Joely shook her head. "No, I've got it covered. I'm going to leave the island. I figure if I get a good enough head start, it'll take him another five years to find me."

Holt gripped the steering wheel so tight, his knuckles turned white.

"That's no life," Mike said. "Always looking over your shoulder."

"It's what I'm used to." Joely turned back around in her seat.

It was her casual acceptance of the situation that infuriated him. There had to be a legal way to solve this so she wasn't indebted to his uncle, and was safe from all harm.

When they got to the ranch, Holt pulled the car inside the garage. Mike hopped out and popped the trunk. "Help me with these," he said, and pulled out two large bags.

"I was planning on finding a hotel by the airport tonight. My flight leaves in the morning, but it looks like I'll be staying here instead," Samantha said.

"Maybe I'll catch a ride with you tomorrow," Joely said.

"Or maybe not," Holt added.

Tetsuo welcomed them inside. Kala met them at the door. "You're back," she said, hugging Holt. "Mike, we were so worried." She hugged her other nephew and then looked at Samantha quizzically.

"Samantha Kane," she said, holding out her hand. "I'm a business associate of your husband."

"It's nice to meet you. Can I get you some dinner? The paniolos just left, but there's still some loco moco. I don't cook fancy, like some people." Kala smiled as she nudged Joely.

"Awesome. I'm starved." Mike hurried into the kitchen.

"We'll be right in," Holt said, nodding to his aunt and Samantha.

When they were gone, he turned to Joely. "We've got a lot to talk about."

"It doesn't matter." She moved to go into the kitchen.

"Damn you, it does."

"I'm leaving in the morning."

"Do you want to?" Holt asked.

Joely stopped in her tracks. "Of course not. I want things to go back the way they were."

"I don't," he said.

He hated the look of hurt that flashed over her face, so he clarified. "Before, we were just friends. I want more."

"That's impossible. We're too different. I could never make you happy," she said, her voice cracking.

"Bullshit. I've never been happier than this last week."

She tried for a laugh, but it came out sounding like a hiccup. "Brah, you need to get out more."

"I will, if you're with me."

Joely shook her head. "I can't do this, Holt. I don't have what Timothy is looking for. If he said he's going to put a contract out on my life, he means it. And only after I'm dead, and he's still being squeezed for cash will he realize that he was wrong."

"Do you know why he's being blackmailed?"

164

"Not this time. Five years ago, I'd say it was because he was taking bribes to vote a certain way. I found out about it while I was …"

Joely paused and Holt immediately thought, "Here comes a lie."

"…looking for something else."

Not quite a lie, but not the entire truth. Something was still going on that she was hiding from him.

"What aren't you telling me?" He took her hand and rubbed his thumb over her knuckles.

"A lot of things. I want you to remember me with happiness. If I told you all my secrets, it would color how you feel about me."

"No, it wouldn't."

"Holt, trust me. I know you, and I know what I'm hiding. You'd hate me."

"I could never hate you."

She gave a short laugh. "You'd call the police on me, then."

"I didn't last night."

"I'm not the girl you want." She turned back to walk into the kitchen.

"Timothy said you were a hacker."

Joely flinched. "I was," she said without turning around.

"Tell me about it."

"There's not enough time."

"I'll make the time." He held out his hand. "Let's go for a walk."

"It's getting dark," she said.

165

"I'll protect you."

"I'm not afraid of the damned dark."

"Then what are you waiting for?"

"Your uncle is expecting us to sit down to dinner with them."

"Then he's going to be disappointed. He roped us into coming here, but he can't control what we do."

"You're a rebel now?" A slow smile crept across her face.

"If you come with me, I'll show you where I used to hide out from my chores when I was a boy."

Holt could see the indecision on her face. He waited. He wouldn't put any more pressure on her. It had to be her choice.

"Fine," she said. "But I'm hungry. I never got my empanadas."

"Go to the stables. I'll meet you there."

Joely rolled her eyes, but she went out the door instead of into the kitchen.

Mike and Samantha were already digging into their meal at the long pine table. Kala and Tetsuo were examining the fridge.

"Excuse me," Holt said, pushing in between them to grab a bag of Hawaiian sweet rolls and some sliced ham.

"Where are you going?" Kala asked.

"Joely and I have some issues to discuss."

"You can discuss them after dinner."

"Auntie, Holt needs to grovel," Mike said.

"Shut it," Holt said, going to the wine rack for a bottle of wine. He juggled everything around in his arms before Kala sighed in exasperation, and opened the cabinet door to hand him the picnic basket.

166

"Why does he need to grovel?" Kala asked.

"He fired Joely."

"Holt," Kala scolded. "Why?"

"It's complicated," Holt said.

"But he redeemed himself by knocking around her ex-husband," Tetsuo said.

"Who has put a contract out on her life," Samantha added.

Kala put her hand to her forehead and sat at the table. "Go. Just go."

"Thank you, Auntie." Holt leaned down and kissed her cheek.

Jogging out to the barn, he was afraid that Joely would have tried to make a run for it, but he saw her in the moonlight.

"I'm not riding a horse at night."

"You won't have to. Come on." He held her hand and led her through the stables to the ladder that led to the hayloft. "Climb up."

"Are you serious?"

"Here, take this blanket if you can. I've got dinner."

"You're lucky I'm hungry," she said.

He followed her up the ladder. Spreading the large blanket over the hay he made the sandwiches while she poured the wine into plastic cups.

"It's not Sunset in Lahaina," Holt said. "But it's home."

They tapped their glasses together, and ate in silence for a while.

"So, you used to hide up here when you were a kid?" Joely said, wiping her mouth on a paper towel.

"I had my stack of comic books over there and a flashlight. I would sneak out after dark and come up here to read."

"It's cozy," she said.

"Better than a shed?"

"Different."

"I'm ready to listen if you want to tell me your secrets."

"It's easier in the dark," she said and switched off the barn lamp. The outline of the bare bulb shone for a bit and then gradually faded.

Holt drained his wine and lay flat on his back. She cuddled in next to him and he put his arms around her. Everything was right in the world. If he had to quit Palekaiko, and take a job here to keep her safe, he would. He was drifting off into a contented sleep when she started talking.

"My parents are professional con artists. Grifters. They excelled in the long con. Low risk, big profits. My brother was their enforcer. Tanner was a big dude that they would use to intimidate people. He was a gentle giant, though. Makoa reminds me a lot of him.

My sisters and I were apprenticed out when we were in elementary school. Katie took martial arts and weaponry. I had a knack for computers, and Sammy went to my uncle to learn how to make counterfeit money and forgeries.

So," she said, propping herself up on her elbow. "Your uncle and my uncle have a lot in common."

Holt was wide awake now. Something was niggling in the back of his mind, but he couldn't figure out what.

"After Tanner died, I wanted out. I couldn't forgive my parents for his death. Then Katie got vengeance and went away for life. I was done. I married the first guy that came along, and you've seen how well that went."

Holt didn't know what to say, but he stroked her hair and back.

"I knew I needed a steady income if I was going to leave Timothy, so I hooked up with a guy who would give me jobs. It started out small. Get the biology final from this professor's laptop. Then it escalated up. The jobs let me sock away a small nest egg, and if I'm being honest, I loved the thrill it gave me to steal." Joely buried her face in his chest.

"You did what you had to do. No one was hurt. Just a few cheaters got a free ride."

"Thanks. That means a lot coming from you." She hugged him. "I also fixed computers on the side and worked in the computer lab, so it wasn't all undercover stuff. But then, a professor approached me. He wanted me to steal a rival professor's thesis project and his lab results on some stupid shit I can't even remember. Petty bullshit, but he promised me a year's tuition and a place to stay for free, so I took him up on it."

"What happened?" Holt prompted her when she didn't say anything else.

She held him tighter. "I broke into his office at night and hacked into his laptop. I got the information I needed and was about to leave when I got greedy. I figured I'd download his class lists, his tests, and see if I could find a buyer. But while I was looking, I found that he was lobbying to get a bill passed. I found that he donated very heavily to my husband's campaign."

"Not a crime."

"No, but finding the email from my husband telling the professor that he needed more money to make it happen otherwise he would vote against it, is."

"That seems awfully stupid that he would put that in writing."

"He thought they were on a secure server. And they were, if it hadn't been for me. So, I downloaded everything I could find on my laptop. I figured if I could corroborate the bribe on Timothy's computer, I could strong arm him into granting me a nice quiet divorce. And maybe a decent alimony payoff. Like I said, I got greedy."

Joely sighed. "When I got home that night, I waited until Timothy was asleep and picked the lock to his office. Yeah, there was a lot more shit on his computer. He had his hands in everyone's pocket. I had enough on him to ruin him."

"You don't have to tell me the rest." Holt could feel her shaking.

"I was cocky. I thought I knew it all, and that Timothy was a dumb son of a bitch. Well, the dumbass had an alert set up to ring his phone when anyone other than him accessed certain files. He caught me. And well, you know the rest."

"You said he destroyed your laptop."

"I thought he did."

"Why does he think you still have it?"

Joely shrugged. "Someone has it. Or at least the data I ripped off of the professor's laptop."

"Do you think it's the professor that's blackmailing him?"

"No, the bribes worked. The bill got passed. It must be someone else Timothy's pissed off."

"Could you find out who?"

"Yeah, it's just a matter of time."

"Then do it. Stay here until you can find out who it is."

"What good will that do?"

"Then we'll call the police. The blackmailer goes to jail, and so does Timothy. We'll make it look like the blackmailer was the one to drop the dime, and we can go on with our lives."

"I don't think anyone drops a dime anymore," she said. "It's more like a quarter. Or they use burner phones or something."

"You know what I mean."

There was more silence, but this time Holt could almost hear her thinking.

"It might work," she said finally.

"Well, that's one problem down. Ready to take on the next one?"

"I think we might need more wine."

"I want you in my life."

He shocked her. Her entire body went stiff.

"Didn't you hear me?" she said. "My family is just like your uncle, only not as successful."

"I want you, not them."

"I don't even know where most of them are, but they could come back and cause trouble, especially if they get wind of the Kincaides."

"We'll handle it. Together."

She swallowed hard. "I've never really had a functional relationship."

"Me neither come to think of it. We'll have to make allowances for that. Forgive each other when we fuck up. I fucked up when I fired you and confiscated the lap top. You might have already figured out who the blackmailer is if I hadn't done that."

Joely shrugged. "Maybe. My skills are rusty and technology has changed a lot. Hacking into Timothy's rig was a piece of cake. Trying to find out the identity of the blackmailer is probably going to be more difficult."

"Do you forgive me?"

"Do you forgive me?" Joely responded.

"Yes."

"Yes," she said, and he could hear the smile in her voice. "So, are we done for tonight or is there another big issue to solve?"

"I think we're good for tonight. Do you want to go back inside?"

"Not just yet."

She sat up and Holt figured she was going to get another glass of wine. But then her fingers were on his waistband and she unbuttoned his slacks.

"What are you doing?" he asked as she pulled down the zipper of his pants.

"Enjoying myself," she said, reaching into his underwear and pulling his cock out.

It was already hard and ready for her. When her mouth lowered down on it, Holt almost lost control. He had not been expecting that. Joely worked his cock in and out of her mouth, sucking and licking him until he was powerless to do anything but moan her name.

She moaned back and the vibrations in her throat were another layer of pleasure against his sensitive nerve endings. Joely splayed her hand under his shirt so she could rub his chest and abs.

"Fuck, baby. Yes."

Holt tangled his fingers in her hair, his hips rose to meet her mouth.

"I'm going to come," he warned her, as his body shook.

Pleasure crashed down on him and when she didn't move away, he held her head to him as the shockwaves lifted him like he was surfing through a pipeline.

"Joely, oh sweet heart," he muttered.

Crawling up his body, she settled on his chest and listened to his pounding heart. "Now, we can go back inside."

"Not yet, we can't."

Holt slowly undressed her. Pulling her shirt over her head, he unhooked her bra. Laying her down on the blanket, he kissed her, tasting himself on her tongue. He felt himself get hard again. As they kissed, he trailed his fingers over her taut nipples and teased trails down to her belly button and back.

When her mouth was hot and her lips swollen for his kisses, Holt nibbled down to her neck. He sought out all her sensitive places and attacked them with his tongue and teeth.

It was her turn to moan his name.

Licking down to her chest, he massaged her breasts and spent a lot of time sucking on her nipples. He loved the little desperate cries she made as he tongued circles around them.

"Please," she moaned. "Fuck me."

"Eventually," he promised and kissed down to her belly button.

He undid the button of her shorts with his teeth and yanked them off her long legs. Taking off her sandals, Holt nibbled at her ankles. He spread her legs wide and knelt between him while he got undressed. Tracing his fingers over her panties, he grinned when he found them drenched. He rubbed the silky material between her legs.

"Do you like the friction?"

"Take them off," she whispered.

"All right." He licked the skin above the waistline and then along the edges of her panties. Unable to wait anymore, Holt pulled them off.

He buried his face between her legs and licked up and down through her hot, wet folds. He French kissed her pussy like it was her mouth, getting lost in her sighs and trembling thighs.

Her hips pumped up to meet his mouth. He cupped her ass and went to work on her clit. Joely cried out so loud, she scared the horses. He sucked on her throbbing bud until she came on his face. Then, he licked her some more.

When his cock felt ready to burst, he raised himself up and fiddled with his pants for the condom.

"Fucking boy scout," she said, breathlessly.

"Come here," he growled. Grabbing her legs, he wrapped them around his waist. Holt rubbed his cock through her wet folds, torturing both of them. He inched in, as she clasped tight around him. It was effortless to slide in deep.

Holt fucked her with long, hard strokes. Joely kissed him, her fingernails digging half-moons into his shoulders. He thrust into her fast, driving deep. He put all his fear, anger and frustration in the relentless pace and she met him stroke for stroke.

Joely came first, her entire body spasming in pleasure. Holt lost words and could only grunt and growl as his own orgasm nearly blinded him with the intensity. And still he couldn't stop. He rocked into her body as she twitched and moaned. Rolling off her, he took in great gulps of air.

"Now, can we go inside? I want to be on top this time and I'm afraid I'll bang my head on the loft."

If she was serious, she was going to be the death of him.

She grabbed hold of his cock.

Joely was serious, and he was going to die a happy man.

Chapter Eighteen

Joely did the walk of shame from the barn. They never got out of the loft and she managed not to bang her head. Although, she was still picking hay out of her hair. The ranch house was dark and Holt kissed her goodnight outside her room.

"Will I see you in the morning?" he asked.

"How does blueberry pancakes sound?" she asked.

"Like there's going to be a lot of happy paniolos."

He kissed her once last time and it was everything she could do to stop herself from begging him to stay with her tonight. But she needed to talk to her sister and find out what's going on.

Joely opened the door to her room, figuring she'd wait an hour or so before searching for Sammy.

"Took you long enough."

Jumping at her sister's voice, Joely held a hand over her heart as she closed the door. Sammy flicked on the light. She had changed into jeans and a T-shirt.

"I'm so happy to see you." Joely hugged her. "How have you been?"

"Life's been good," she said. "Not living on a beach and banging a hottie like that good, but I get by."

"Well, the sex is a new development."

"I've got your papers." Sammy reached in to a tote bag, and pulled out a driver's license and a passport. "You're Vicky Tanner."

Joely looked up at her sister. She used brother's name.

Sammy shrugged. "I'm getting sentimental in my old age."

"Thanks for these." Joely put them back in the tote bag. "How much?"

"How about we work out a little trade. Mike tells me you're back in business."

"I'm not. I just did it to keep tabs on Timothy. Besides, I don't even have a computer."

Samantha handed her a briefcase.

"What's this?" Joely asked. But she knew. It was probably a state-of-the-art laptop. She sat down at the vanity and stared at it.

"Open it up," Sammy said impatiently.

She really shouldn't, but if it would help her find out who the blackmailer was, it would be worth it. With shaking fingers, she opened the briefcase.

"I don't believe it," Joely said, blinking and doing a double take.

An eerie alien's head peered up at her.

"Is this?"

"Yup. It's your laptop. I upgraded the video card and the memory."

Joely closed the briefcase. "You're the one blackmailing Timothy."

"Of course, I am. Do you think I was going to let that mother fucker get away with what he did to you?"

"So, we're going to give him this and any copies you made, right?" Joely turned to her sister.

"Or we can get the fuck out of Dodge and keep it up until the fat bastard dies of a stroke." Sammy clapped her hands together in

177

glee. "Mom and Dad have a whale on a hook down in Australia. We can go there and help out for a while. Make some cash and tour the world. Hey, they surf down there. Maybe you can find another hottie that's not so tight assed."

"Holt isn't… okay, yeah he's a tight ass. But he's a good man."

Sammy made a face. "Bo-oring."

"I like boring," Joely realized. "I don't want your crazy life."

"You've gone respectable?" Sammy snorted.

"Yeah."

"I think you're just too into the role you've been playing for the past five years. You can't stay here. You'd make it easy for Timothy's hit squad. Unless you want to make a deal with Mr. Hojo."

Joely shook her head. "I'm not getting involved with him."

"You're banging his nephew. I think you're a little bit connected."

"Holt doesn't want anything to do with anything criminal."

"His brother doesn't have that point of view."

"Yeah, Mike is different. How do you know Mike and Tetsuo?"

"Mr. Hojo is a client. Mike started out as a potential business partner, but he's too much of a loose cannon. And I found out tonight that he's backed by an organized crime family so I've got a nine a.m. flight. I've got a ticket for you too. First class to Sydney."

Joely knew that nothing was free. She would be paying for her papers and the first-class flight through hacking and other illegal activities. Five years ago, she would have jumped at the chance. She would have been full of outrage and the need for vengeance. And she probably would have destroyed her life, like Katie did.

"Thank you, but I can't. My life is here."

"Your life is over. Unless you can stop Timothy."

Joely pointed to the laptop. "Is this the only copy of the evidence?"

"Of course not."

"I need you to get it for me."

"No way. Have you forgotten everything Mom and Dad taught us?"

"I tried to, yeah."

"Someone is always going to screw you over. You hand that over to Timothy, what's to say he won't try to kill you after all? Because he promised? Do you fucking trust that asshole?"

"No."

"Then why would you give up all your leverage?"

She had a point. "Will you let me keep the laptop and will you promise not to blackmail Timothy ever again?"

Sammy sighed. "What's in it for me? I'm losing a lot of money if I do that."

Joely looked at her feet. "I can pay you. Installments. Out of every check."

"What do you take home? A couple of grand a month? Tops? Annie, that doesn't pay my bar tab."

"What do you want? For the laptop. You can keep the papers."

Sammy waved her hand. "Keep the papers. I can't reuse them and you're going to need them. You're just too stupid in love with that hunky boy scout to see that."

Was she?

Joely took a deep, shuddering breath. Yeah, for about five years now. She waited, letting Sammy name the price so they could negotiate it.

"I want a favor from you. One a year for the rest of our lives."

"No problem, as long as it's legal."

Sammy hissed between her teeth. "I don't need a lot of help in that regard. I'm looking for things that skate the line a little."

"No can do. I'm out of that life."

"What if it was more white hat work instead of black hat?"

She narrowed her eyes. "What do you mean?"

"What if I'm the Robin Hood of expeditors. We rob from the rich and corrupt and give to the victims and the needy."

Joely thought about it for a bit. "I'd have to research each job to determine if it's on the up and up. I reserve the right to deny a favor."

"You can refuse, but you'd owe me two favors."

"If my research turns out that it's illegal, I'm off the hook for a favor for that year."

They glared at each other for a few moments.

"Deal," Sammy said, holding out her hand.

"You're going to stop blackmailing Timothy?"

She nodded. "But I'm keeping copies in case of any fuckery on his part. However, I swear to you I won't use it unless he renegs on his part."

Joely shook her hand. "You got a deal."

"I should get my things. I'd rather not sleep here. I'll doze at my gate."

"How are you going to get to the airport?"

"I called an Uber."

Joely smacked her forehead. "I should have done that instead of taking the Jaguar with Mike."

"You need to think things through a little more. Stop reacting." She opened the door and walked out in the hall.

Joely didn't want her to go. Not yet. She followed her into the other guest room.

"Is there something you want me to say to Mom and Dad when I see them?"

Crossing to the window, Joey looked out into the night. The stars were out and there was a fresh hint of lavender in the air. "Tell them I'm not mad anymore. Tell them I've found my place and that I'm happy. But let them know that I'm a civilian now. I'm out of their crazy life."

"Yeah, I think they know the last part. But they'll be glad to hear the first part of that. You know how to reach us, if you need us."

Joely hugged her. "If you need me, just call."

"I will. Once a year, at least."

They shared a quiet laugh. Joely helped carry one of her sister's suitcases downstairs.

She dropped it when she saw who was waiting in the foyer.

Timothy and Tetsuo looked up at the loud thud.

Chapter Nineteen

"Holt!" Joely screamed. "Help!"

"There's no need for that," Tetsuo said. "He's not here for you. There's your blackmailer. The same person who was spying on my computer."

"What?" Joely whipped her head to her sister.

Holt came thundering down the stairs.

"I should have known you two bitches were working together," Timothy snarled.

"Uncle, what have you done?" Holt said.

"I believe you're in error, Senator. Samantha Kane worked alone. Our Joely had no knowledge that you were being blackmailed."

"You expect me to believe she didn't put her sister up to it?" Timothy snarled.

Tetsuo blinked, and then narrowed his gaze on Joely and Sammy.

"Sisters?" Holt said coming up behind her.

"This is my sister, Sammy. Look, I can make this right," Joely said. "My old laptop is upstairs. It's on the vanity. I'll just go get it."

"No, you stay the fuck here," Timothy said. "Let lover boy go get it."

"Holt, it's in the briefcase on the vanity."

Holt didn't say a word, but took the stairs two at a time.

"What's all this noise?" Kala said, storming out of her bedroom, wrapping her robe around her.

"Go back to bed."

She glared at them. "Tetsuo, I warned you about bringing business home. I'm leaving for Wailea tomorrow. I've had it." She turned on her heel and marched back into her room.

Holt came back downstairs, carrying the briefcase. "Here," he said, stuffing it into Timothy's hands.

Timothy placed it on the side table and opened it up. "What's that?"

Holt held the envelope containing her new passport and identification. He handed it to Joely. "Holt, I can explain."

He wouldn't look at her.

"Are those copies of the evidence?" Timothy asked.

Joely slid out the passport and driver's license, being careful not to let him see the name on it.

"See what a treacherous bitch she is?"

"You're going to stop using that word," Holt warned.

Timothy glared at him, rubbing his jaw. "Where are the copies?"

"Destroyed," Joely said, reaching down to hold her sister's hand.

"Am I supposed to believe that?" he said.

"Am I supposed to believe you're not going to try to kill me, once all my leverage is gone?"

Timothy smirked. "You're a smart bitch." He pulled out a pistol and pointed it at her.

183

"You dare?" Tetsuo said, stepping in front of Joely even as Holt shoved her behind him.

Joely yanked Sammy behind Holt as well.

"Our deal was I provide the blackmailer to you," Tetsuo ground out. "I welcomed you into our home, and this is how you repay my good will?"

"I don't deal with gangsters or thugs."

"For the right price you will," Joely said.

"You watch your smart mouth. Now, I'm going to start shooting. If you want to avoid a lot of dead bodies, you and your bitch of a sister are coming with me. I want every dime you skimmed from me."

"Go to hell," Sammy said.

"You first." He raised the gun.

"I lied," Joely said, quickly.

"There's a big surprise," Timothy said.

"I kept a copy of the evidence. It's in a safe deposit box in Australia. Upon the death of me or my sister, my parents open it up and set that shit free. Every dirty deal you did. Every bribe you took. The world is going to know. Your life will be ruined. The Feds will be all over you."

"You're lying," Timothy said.

Joely forced her breathing to be still and with an iron will spoke so her voice didn't shake. She was bluffing her ass off right now.

"You don't have to believe her. You're a dead man either way," Sammy said.

"I'm the one with the gun, you little bitch."

"Do you know what the *ninkyo dankai* are?" Sammy asked.

184

"This is America. I speak English."

"You're familiar with the mafia, I'm assuming?"

"No comment."

"Well, you're holding a gun on the boss of this island."

Timothy blinked at stared at Tetsuo. He took a step back. One hand held the pistol steady, the other snapped the briefcase closed.

"This isn't over." Timothy said, grabbing the briefcase in one hand. His gun hand never wavered. He walked backwards towards the door. Placing the briefcase down, Timothy reached back for the door knob.

When he opened it, Joely saw Mike behind him. Somehow, he had been outside and was waiting for Timothy.

Holt squeezed her hand, and she forced herself to keep her eyes on Timothy so as not to give away Mike's advantage. When Timothy bent down to pick up the briefcase, Mike attacked.

Things happened fast. Mike yanked Timothy's gun to the left and smashed his foot into his knee. A shot rang out. Holt dove for the floor taking Joely and her sister with him. He covered them with his body.

From the back of the house, Kala screamed.

There was a brief scuffle. The vase on the side table crashed on the ground. There were grunts of pain and the heavy sounds of fists hitting flesh.

Kala rounded the corner with a shotgun and racked it. The sound of the bullet ejecting from the chamber was almost as loud as a gunshot.

Everything stopped.

"Get that haole piece of shit out of my house," Kala said.

Joely hoped she wasn't referring to her.

Chapter Twenty

Holt drove Samantha to the airport so she could catch her flight. Joely was in the car as well, and he wasn't sure if she was planning on using her new identification and leaving with her sister or not.

He couldn't bring himself to ask. It was a strained and quiet ride. Pulling into short term parking, he helped Samantha with her bags to the shuttle bus station where they stood around awkwardly.

"Holt, can you give us a few minutes?" Joely asked.

"Sure." Holt went back to his car and leaned against it. He really couldn't blame her if she took off. He wasn't sure what was going to happen to Timothy, but he hoped his uncle wouldn't assassinate a United States senator. On the other hand, drownings happened every day.

He watched them talk. Now that he knew they were sisters, he could see the resemblance. And now it made perfect sense why she was talking about Timothy in front of her.

When the shuttle bus pulled up, every muscle tensed in Holt's body. He fought the urge to run back to her and beg her to stay. After one last hug, though, Joely stepped back.

Samantha looked at him and waved. He waved back.

Joely watched the bus take off and drive toward the terminal. He started breathing again when she walked up to him and rested her head on his chest.

"I can explain the passport."

He gave a short laugh. "You don't have to."

"It was my back up plan. If things went to shit and if Timothy couldn't be stopped. I could get away."

"I understand."

"I decided not to use them though after talking with you in the hayloft."

"We did more than talk, wahine." The fear loosened in his chest. Tucking a stray strand of hair behind her ear, he leaned down and kissed her.

"Nothing's changed for me, Holt." She held his hand. "But I understand if you don't want any part of me or my family."

"I kinda know where you're coming from on relatives that cross the legal lines. If you don't hold it against me, I won't hold it against you."

"Deal," she said, and stood up on tiptoe to give him a kiss.

There were probably better places to make out. On top of Haleakala. On Kaanapali Beach. Hell, even on a surf board waiting for a wave. But there wasn't anywhere Holt wanted to be right now.

"What happens now?" Joely asked.

"We still got a few more days of vacation left. And you did promise the guys clam chowder."

"I can stay at the ranch until Timothy leaves?" She grinned.

"And then it's back to work at Palekaiko. You okay with that?"

"More than okay."

He opened the car door for her and turned to look one last time at the shuttle bus before getting into the car himself.

"What do you think Tetsuo is going to do to Timothy?"

"I think that all depends on how willing Timothy is to make amends."

Epilogue

One Year Later

Kala and Sammy were fussing with her lei.

"It's fine," Joely said.

She was barefoot and wore a white sundress. Holt had insisted she wear this huge white hat with the big brim so she wasn't lobster red by the time the ceremony ended.

"I don't know why you didn't want to get married at one of Tetsuo's properties," Kala sniffed, bobby pinning her veil onto the hat.

"We wanted it to be at the resort."

"Because you two don't spend enough time here," Sammy said.

Joely picked out an Aloha patterned dress for her with bright red hibiscus flowers and splashes of purple lavender leaves on a cream background. Sammy was also barefoot.

Kala, of course, was in an evening gown and three inch heels. Joely wasn't sure how she was going to walk on the beach in those, but she had other things to worry about.

"Is Dude sober?" she asked Sammy.

Sammy shrugged. "How can you tell?"

She had a point.

Amelia and Michaela came in, dressed the same as Sammy.

"They're almost ready for you," Amelia said, handing her an iced glass of pog.

"Marcus made Dude promise to behave," Michaela said, giving her a quick hug.

"Is everybody getting along out there?" Joely asked.

"So far so good. Holt hasn't hit his father. Dude and Marcus haven't gotten into a screaming match with Tetsuo. And the band is sober." Amelia gave her a shaka.

Makoa had arranged for the music. He was going to play the steel drums. Hani and Kai were on ukuleles and Mel was going to sing.

Holt probably would have preferred that his father not show up at all, which was why Makoa made him part of the band.

That and Mel was taking on more responsibility at Palekaiko, now that Holt was only working there part time. They split their days working part of the week at the ranch and part of the week at the resort.

It was the best of both worlds. Joely knew that they would have to choose eventually. But for right now, Tetsuo was satisfied that Holt was training to be foreman and would take over once Joe retired. And while Joely knew her heart would always call this resort home, she was looking forward to her new adventure Upcountry.

But not for a couple of more years yet.

She couldn't help comparing today with her first wedding ceremony. Instead of being on a beach at sunset, surrounded by friends and family, Joely had stood in too tight shoes and wore a rented suit dress while standing in front of a justice of the peace. Joely didn't remember feeling anything but relieved. She certainly didn't feel like her heart was going to burst from love, like she did today.

Timothy was out of her life for good. And after today, when she said the word husband, it would only mean Holt.

Over the past year, Joely used her remote access to monitor Timothy's correspondence. There hadn't been a single mention of her. She wasn't sure what transpired between Tetsuo and Timothy, while Holt took Sammy to the airport that day, but it had been enough to scare him away.

However, he still sexted Cami and shared videos with her, which Joely wouldn't open even if her life depended on it. She also found out by spying on their non-sexual chats that it was obvious that Cami was on Tetsuo's payroll. And so was Timothy. Or at least, if he wasn't getting a paycheck from Tetsuo, his continued existence was how he was being compensated for his cooperation.

While Holt wanted to fire Cami on the spot, Amelia and Joely convinced him that it would help them control the information they wanted Tetsuo to have. It was always better to know who the snitch was than not.

When Makoa pounded out the first couple of bars of *Here Comes the Bride*, Joely got a case of butterflies in her stomach.

"They're playing your song," Sammy said.

Linking arms with Kala and Sammy, Joely walked out of the pavilion and into the sun. Amelia and Michaela followed, carrying thick bouquets of plumeria and roses. After a few sinking steps in the sand, Kala cursed and kicked off her shoes.

Their guests stood on either side of the makeshift aisle. At the end of the walkway, Holt looked confident and sure of himself standing next to Dude and Mike.

Mike looked nervous.

Dude smirked.

She smiled back at him, her nerves fleeing into the wind.

As the waves crashed down, soft ukulele music played until she stood next to Holt.

"You look beautiful," he said, removing the veil and kissing her.

"Hey," Dude said. "That's not until da end of the program, bruddah. Take it easy."

Holt rolled his eyes.

Dude took a swig of his Cerveza and cleared his throat.

"I think I speak for everyone here, that it's about fucking time these two tied the knot."

There were a few whoops and cheers at that.

"Wahine, dis guy has had hearts in his eyes from the moment he saw you. Brah," Dude turned to Holt. "You could have tripped over her tongue every time you walked by with a surfboard."

Joely sighed. He wasn't wrong. But it was still embarrassing.

"Do you love her?"

"With all my heart," Holt said.

Joely's eyes grew misty, and she leaned her cheek against his arm.

"What about you, Sistah?"

"I love him too."

"Well, that's the easy part. There's going to be a lot of outside forces gonna want to tear that apart. Whether it's because of jealousy or because Fate is a fickle bitch. But you've got each other, so you're already ahead of the game. Got it?"

Joely nodded.

"Holt, do you promise not to be a pin head and fire this girl when she gets into trouble."

"Uh, I do?"

"Joely, do you promise to involve Holt in all your harebrained schemes."

"Sure, yeah. I guess." She grinned up at him.

"K'den. Hey parrot head, you up. Give me the rings."

Mike jolted and tapped his pockets before pulling out two simple gold bands. Dude took them from him and handed him a wooden bowl filled with water.

"For you guys in the cheap seats, this here is a Koa wood bowl. I dipped it into the ocean a few minutes ago. That symbolizes me washing away anything that's in the past. This is a fresh start. Their future comes brand new from the ocean, clean and pure." Dude held up a leaf. "This is a Ti leaf." He dropped it into the bowl and swirled it around in the water. "Koa is a hardwood. That represents a strong foundation for your marriage. The leaf is a symbol of island life. It represents good fortune and blessings of happiness."

Dude cupped some of the water in his hand and sprinkled it over the rings.

"Ei-Ah Eha-No. Ka Malohia Oh-Na-Lani. Mea A-Ku A-Pau." He chanted that a few times.

Holt leaned in and whispered in her ear. "He's saying, may peace from above rest upon you and remain with you now and forever."

"Say it aloud for the crowd, big guy," Dude said.

Holt repeated himself, and the guests clapped.

"Take these." Dude handed them each other's ring.

"Joely, this is your last chance. If you run now, I'll trip him so you can get away."

"No way," she said.

"Good. Put the ring on his finger and say the words."

Joely held Holt's hand. "Today, I'm marrying my best friend. My lover. And my heart's desire. Thank you for accepting me for who I am, flaws and all. And showing me that I deserve to be loved." She slid the ring on his finger.

"Hold on a minute. Sand got in my eye." Dude wiped his face on his sleeve. "Your turn," he said to Holt.

"Today, I'm marrying the love of my life. The one who makes me smile, think, and laugh. I can't wait to grow old with you and share every day with my beautiful wife. *Aloha wau ia oe.*"

Joely's hand was shaking when he pushed the ring on her finger.

"Okay, now you can kiss her. But make it quick. We want to hit the buffet and open bar.

Joely leapt into his arms as Makoa and the boys struck up The Hawaiian Wedding Song, *Ke Kali Nei Au.* Mel even sounded a little like Elvis Presley when he crooned out the words.

The End

Thank you for reading!

– Jamie

193

Links

To learn more about the great island of Maui and what it offers, check out these links:

Maui Guidebook

http://mauiguidebook.com/beaches/hookipa-beach-park/

How to talk like a surfer

http://www.surfing-waves.com/surf_talk.htm

What's that word mean?

http://www.howtoliveinhawaii.com/1023/35-hawaiian-words-every-new-resident-should-know/

Glossary

Did you read a word and wondered what it meant?

'A'ole pilikia – You're welcome / No problem.

Aloha – Has a lot of meanings, but most commonly used as hello, good-bye, and for love.

Aloha wau ia oe – I love you.

Choke – a lot.

Haole – Foreigner, usually used to describe a white tourist.

Keiki – Child.

Lilikoi – Hawaiian passion fruit.

Motobaik – Motorcycle, literally motor bike.

Ninkyo dankai – Japanese for chivalrous organization. It's how the Yakuza, a Japanese organized crime syndicate, refer to themselves.

Ono Grindz – Delicious food.

Poke – ahi or yellow tail tuna, avocado, onion salad. Sometimes made with rice. Here's a good recipe: https://www.huffingtonpost.com/2014/07/21/how-to-make-poke-bowl_n_5593812.html

Roger dat – Literally *Roger That* from radio code "R" meaning received and under stood.

Saimin – a broth based noodle soup made with either ramen or soba noodles. Here's a good recipe: https://www.saveur.com/g00/article/Recipes/Saimin

Shaka – a hand sign made by folding your three middle fingers down, with your pinkie and thumb sticking out and shaking it from side-to-side. Like aloha, it's used in many situations and has more than one meaning, but it's most commonly used to mean "hang loose" or as a thank you.

Here's a fun article about it: https://www.hawaiimagazine.com/content/ho-brah-here-are-7-ways-throw-shaka

Shootz – Yes, sure, you got it.

Wahine – a girl.

Wilwil – two-wheel bicycle.

Yurt – Pavilion tent.

Can't get enough of the Palekaiko Beach Resort? The gang returns in Beauty and the Beach in the July 2018 Skinny Dippy Optional anthology. Makoa falls in love with a mermaid with a secret.

FREE BOOK

Thank you! I hope you enjoyed this book and would consider leaving me a review.

If you'd like to keep up-to-date on my new releases and other fun things, please subscribe to my newsletter and get a *FREE BOOK*.

Be a VIP Reader and have a chance to win monthly prizes, free books and up-to-date information.

Your Free Book:

Click Here:

https://dl.bookfunnel.com/w9gnkxp12u

More Books by Jamie K. Schmidt

If you liked this book, you may want to try:

Three Sisters Ranch Series
(high heat contemporary romance)

USA Today Best Seller: The Cowboy's Daughter

The Cowboy's Hunt

The Cowboy's Heart

A Cowboy for April

A Cowboy for June

A Cowboy for Merry – coming soon

Club Inferno Series
(erotic contemporary romance)

USA Today Best Seller: Heat

Longing

Fever

Passion – coming 2022

The Emerging Queens Series

(high heat paranormal romance)

The Queen's Mystery – FREE when you sign up to be a VIP reader

The Queen's Wings

The Queen's Plight

The Queen's Flight

The Queen's Dance

The Queen's Gambit – coming soon

The Queen's Conclave – coming soon

The Truth & Lies Series

(erotic New Adult romance)

Truth Kills

Truth Reveals

The Hawaii Heat series

(high heat contemporary romance)

USA Today Best Seller: Life's a Beach

Beach Happens

Beach My Life

Beauty and the Beach

The Sentinels of Babylon series
(high heat contemporary romance)

Necessary Evil

Sentinel's Kiss

Warden's Woman

Ryder's Reckoning

Stand-alone novels
(high heat contemporary romance)

2018 Rita® Finalist in Erotic Romance: Stud – Retitled *Extra Whip*

Hard Cover

Maiden Voyage

Spice - Book Three in the Fate Series - Co-written with Jenna Jameson

Wild Wedding Hookup

Holiday Hookup

Stand-alone novels & novellas

Trinity (erotic ménage paranormal romance)

Midnight Lady, (high heat fantasy romance)

Naked Truth (romantic suspense)

Santa Genie (erotic paranormal romance)

Samurai's Heart (erotic paranormal romance)

Betrayed (erotic fantasy romance)

The Handy Men (erotic ménage romance)

Shifter's Price (erotic ménage dystopian paranormal romance)

The Seeker (paranormal romance)

A Spark of Romance (sweet small town romance)

Newsletter Subscriber's First Peek

A Casual Christmas (contemporary romance) – Exclusive to newsletter subscribers for 2017. Now available.

A Not So Casual Christmas (contemporary romance) – Exclusive to newsletter subscribers for 2018. Now available.

A Chaotic Christmas (contemporary romance) – Exclusive to newsletter subscribers for 2019. Now available.

A Second Chance Christmas (contemporary romance) – Exclusive to newsletter subscribers for 2020. Now available.

The Gingerbread Cowboy – Exclusive to newsletter subscribers for 2021. Available wide in October 2022.

Sign up here www.jkschmidt.com/newsletter to receive the 2022 short story The Candy Cane Cowboy FREE on Christmas

Eve. It will be exclusive to newsletter subscribers until October 2023.

Anthologies & Collections

Graveyard Shift (High heat paranormal romance)

Flash Magic (No heat at all speculative fiction stories)

Made in the USA
Las Vegas, NV
02 August 2024

93292129R00121